BARE
FACTS

BARE FACTS

KATHERINE GARBERA

KENSINGTON PUBLISHING CORP.
http://www.kensingtonbooks.com

For Rob

The light in my life
The love in my heart
The man of my dreams

Acknowledgments

Special thanks to Mary Louise Wells for reading the first chapter of this book when I was in desperate need of someone to.

Also thanks to Rob Elser for answering every question I had even when he was at work! And for brainstorming ideas with me when I hit a wall.

And thanks to Krissie O. for pointing me in the right direction for Yakuza research books and for sharing her enthusiasm for all things Japanese with me. Sorry the hero isn't Japanese but the bad guy is!

And lastly a huge thanks to Beverly Brandt and Eve Gaddy—having friends like you makes me realize how blessed I truly am.

Chapter One

To train the mind, you must exercise the patience
and determination it takes to shape that steel.
—The Dalai Lama

Charity Keone wasn't in the best mood as she entered the offices of Liberty Investigations, and reading that quote on the back of the Celestial Seasonings Raspberry Zinger tea box did nothing to improve her thinking. Normally she and the Dalai Lama were simpatico, but nothing Zen was happening for her today.

Instead she wanted to make her way down to the training room and beat the crap out of a punching bag while pretending it was Senator Perry Jones. He might be "for the people," but he could be such a pig. And she wasn't exactly sure what it said about her that she thought he might be her Mr. Right.

She didn't need to see herself in the mirror to know that her looks were a big part of why Perry had thought she'd say yes to being his trophy wife. Of course, he'd worded it more nicely than that, but she'd been considered a sex trophy since she turned fourteen and landed on the cover of *Seventeen*.

It didn't even matter that Perry had seen more to her than the model looks. She'd been his bodyguard last year when he'd been receiving threats because of his liberal politics, and then a few months later had become his fiancée. He refused to acknowledge she was more than her pretty face. Had actually told her that once she became Mrs. Senator Jones, then she could chill out on the Jennifer Garner/Sydney Bristow, *Alias*, wannabe. *As if.*

Sydney Bristow wished she could do all the things that Charity had done on the job. Protecting diplomats, heads of state, and celebrities wasn't exactly a job for the weak-minded.

There was a noise behind her and she glanced over her shoulder just as her coworker Justine O'Neill entered the room.

"Are you going to pour yourself a cup of tea or just keep glaring at the box?" Justine asked.

Charity grabbed a coffee mug from the cabinet and added the tea bag. *Train the mind. Whatever.* She poured hot water over the bag. "I got the text-message from Sam telling me he had a new assignment for us."

"Anna's setting up in the conference room. And we've got five minutes until the call comes in. So spill it."

"Not much to tell. Perry and I broke up." She really tried to keep her voice neutral because despite all the anger she was channeling into her cup of tea, she was also a tad bit hurt. And she didn't want Justine to see that.

"I thought you were going all the way to the finish line with this one."

So had she. "Some of us aren't meant for the white gown and lace veil."

"I'm not, because I've done time—but you're a different story."

"No, I'm not," she said, leaving the kitchen area and heading down the hall to the conference room.

The room was probably a little more high-tech than most. There were three oversize leather chairs, each facing a large flat-screen video monitor at the end of the room. Anna and Justine took their seats sitting side by side and leaving the chair nearest the door for her. The other women sat forward in their leather chairs to gaze at the flat-screen video monitor.

"Coldplay" blared from the speakers of Anna's laptop. The rest of the laptops, one per chair, had the official Liberty Investigations logo on their screens.

No donuts in sight. Conferences at Liberty Investigations were all about business, not about sugar. Too bad. An éclair would do a hell of a lot to improve her mood.

"Hey, Charity. How was last night?" Anna asked.

"Let's not go there."

"That good?"

The ringing of the phone interrupted the conversation and Justine hit the speaker button.

If anyone had told Charity ten years ago she'd be working for a high-tech security outfit with a boss who communicated by speakerphone, she would have thought that person was on drugs. Sam Liberty was no Charlie. And no one would have called any of his employees angels.

She scoffed and stirred her tea. If this were a real-life *Charlie's Angels*, she'd be driving a souped-up Mustang instead of her sensible, late-model sedan. Plus, real security experts didn't chase the bad guys in stilettos, she thought, glancing down at her own modest heeled boots.

"Everyone ready to get the download?"

"Yes, Sam."

Charity focused on the screen of her computer, watching the scrolling information downloading on her screen. On the surface she, Justine, and Anna had absolutely nothing in common. Justine had murdered her lecherous stepfather about the same time that Charity was hitting the newsstands on that *Seventeen* cover. Justine had street smarts and the kind of skills that couldn't be taught in any classroom. Sam had found her working as a bouncer in a dive bar somewhere in Alabama and brought her in to join the team.

Anna on the other hand, was all proper British-lady manners. She'd been officially trained by MI-5, and her path to Liberty Investigations was a mystery to Charity. Anna didn't talk about whatever had happened in London that had led her to Washington, D.C.

"Daniel Williams is our new client. He's the CEO of Williams International—an import/export company based in Seattle and Hong Kong."

Two pictures flashed up on her screen. Charity felt a jolt as she looked at him. Lust at first sight—not exactly what she'd been expecting today. Never before had she felt an instant connection to anyone like Daniel Williams. He was a good-looking man, but more than that, he was smart, savvy, and, from all accounts, ruthless when it came to business.

But what drew her was his eyes. Despite being dressed in suave GQ style, there was an untamed savageness in his eyes that penetrated to her very soul. This man would never call her a wannabe. There was something in his eyes that told her he could see past the surface flash to the substance she never tried to hide.

She rubbed the back of her neck. She must be more tired than she'd realized if she was reacting this way to a photo.

"Normal spellings on the name?" Anna asked, her fingers moving over the keyboard of her laptop.

"Yes, Anna. Williams International is the third-largest importer of goods from Japan to the United States. Daniel has been receiving threats for the last six months. Last night his home was invaded and his household staff roughed up. The housekeeper is in the hospital."

"What kind of threats?" Charity asked.

"Death threats and blackmail. The files I'm sending you will explain everything. Charity, you will serve as a bodyguard to Mr. Williams. Justine and Anna, I want the both of you to dig deep and find out who the blackmailer is."

Charity nodded, tearing herself away from Daniel's piercing gaze. Business, she reminded herself. Time to do what she did best—kick ass. "No problem. When do I leave for Seattle?"

"It's not going to be a piece of cake," Sam Liberty said via a voice box on the desk. She'd never actually met her boss but that didn't stop her from respecting the hell out of him.

Of course, it helped that he'd always treated her as a respected member of the team, and not a piece of arm candy.

Sam was the boss of her three-person team. They only took on clients that Sam approved of, and operated all over the world.

Death threats, she thought, but the guy was a CEO, and Charity doubted she'd be going up against a military-trained sniper. "You're the boss."

"That's right, I am. Mr. Williams is actually in D.C. on business, so you'll meet him at his suite at the Marquis. You'll be flying to Seattle via his private jet."

"Is the pilot someone we know or one of his people?" Charity asked.

"His. Let's make checking out the jet and pilot our first priority," Sam said.

"I'm on it," Justine said.

"That's all for now."

All three women stood up and started toward the door. Charity was already trying to decide how to handle the bodyguard routine. There were a lot of uber-wealthy people in the Seattle area, so she'd worked there before as a bodyguard and was familiar with the layout of the city.

"Charity, I'd like a word with you."

Justine and Anna kept walking and Charity stopped, waiting until the door closed to turn back around.

"You okay?" Sam asked. There was a state-of-the-art video camera in the room so Sam could see them.

"Sure, why are you asking?"

"Word reached me that you broke off your engagement with Senator Jones last night."

Great. "It's not a big deal. We just discovered we wanted different things from marriage."

"Both of you discovered?"

"I don't pry into your personal life," she said.

"Enough said. But I worry about you, Charity. You live only half a life."

"I'm happiest when I'm working."

"I've had the feeling lately that you are getting bored," Sam said.

She was, but not with work. That was partially what bothered her about breaking up with Perry. It didn't hurt nearly as much as it would have if she'd loved the man. "I'm not."

"It's okay to ask for some time off."

What the hell would she do with time off? "I don't need it. I think guarding Daniel Williams will be exactly what I need."

"He's not just a pretty face," Sam said.

"You don't need to tell me that," she said. She always looked beyond the surface. Never took anything at face value because she herself was so much more than what the world saw.

Charity flipped through the file, skimming the details about Daniel Williams. He was urbane and sophisticated but his file also showed that he had a hidden side. A side that the public and his shareholders would find rather uncomfortable, a side that was shrouded in mystery. There was no information on Daniel Williams until he turned twenty-eight and started his importation business.

"What do you think?" Sam asked.

Charity glanced up at the voice box and knew that saying no, that turning down this bodyguard mission simply wasn't an option.

She didn't want to guard this man. There was something disturbing in his eyes. Even in a damned photograph.

"Why does he need us? People like Daniel Williams have their own security force. This sounds like some kind of white-collar crime."

"Two people are in the hospital. The housekeeper is in critical condition. He wants to set himself up as bait to catch the people behind the attacks," Sam said.

The mission specs were simple. Normally this was exactly the type of assignment that she loved.

"Charity?"

She knew what Sam was asking without hearing another word. She took a deep breath, trying to ignore the feeling in her gut that said this was a mistake, then reminded herself he was just a man and probably not as good-looking in person.

"I'll make sure he stays alive while we find out who is threatening him."

Daniel Williams had made some piss-poor decisions in his life. Of course, anyone who went from a street kid with gang connections to the owner of a billion-dollar international company was bound to make a few mistakes.

Sitting in the living room area of his suite and waiting for his bodyguard to arrive seemed like one of the most ridiculous decisions he'd ever made. He knew how to handle a gun. And he knew who was blackmailing him. What he hadn't been able to do was find Sekijima. One time he'd been the Gashira to Sekijima's Oyabun, but now they were mortal enemies. He fingered the missing joint on his right hand—his index finger was short and misshapen from a past mistake.

So he'd gone to Liberty Investigations. Sam Liberty was one of those names he'd heard off and on for years, a shadowy figure who knew how to get a job done well within the law.

He rubbed the back of his neck, wishing for a moment he wasn't the CEO, but still a street thug with more guts than smarts. Then he'd go to one of Sekijima's warehouses and leave only when he had the answers he wanted. Like where the hell was the bastard hiding.

But nowadays he had a board of directors to answer to, and stockholders who got a little panicky about seeing the CEO of their company wielding a gun.

Daniel had been willing to wait out the threats and try to bait Sekijima into doing something stupid, but instead Mildred, his housekeeper, had been attacked and hospitalized. Alonzo, one of the team of security men that worked for his company, opened the door and came in.

"Charity Keone from Liberty Investigations is outside, Mr. Williams. Is she expected?"

"Yes, show her in."

Charity. What the hell kind of name was that for a body-guard?

The door opened and the sunlight from the floor-to-ceiling windows on the left side of the room cast a shadow around the doorway so that he saw her emerge slowly. First a pair of sexy boots that ended at her calf. The smooth expanse of her slim legs extended to her upper thigh where they disappeared beneath the hem of her slim-fitting black miniskirt. He skimmed his gaze over her blousy vee-neck top. Her breasts were large—at least a D-cup—and the material clung to them. A pendant at her neck nestled an inch above her cleavage.

It took some effort to pull his gaze away from her body. When he did, he looked into a pair of serious gunmetal-gray eyes. He cleared his throat as he got to his feet.

The eyes pierced through him for a second. There was something lethal in her gaze that promised him that she was more than capable of whatever job she set her mind to. It was an expression he'd learned to wear at an early age, but she didn't look as if she'd grown up rough. She looked like she'd grown up in a rich man's house. The kind of place where she would have been pampered and had her every need taken care of. So why the hard-assed gaze?

"Ms. Keone?" he asked.

"Yes, Mr. Williams. Have a seat and we can talk about your security needs."

The only needs on his mind right now involved removing her clothing. But that wasn't going to happen. Not yet, anyway. For now, he had to get his head back into this game.

If Sekijima could see him now he'd realize that blackmail

wasn't necessary to bring him to his knees. Only this five-foot-seven-inch woman.

"I don't know—"

"Don't let my appearance fool you, Mr. Williams. Have you had a chance to look at my credentials?"

He had. She was impressive on paper, but he was having a very hard time reconciling that with the woman who stood before him.

"Of course I have," he said, pacing away from her to face the windows that looked out over the D.C. skyline, which he'd be glad to abandon for Seattle and his view of Puget Sound. Two days of testifying before a house subcommittee made him claustrophobic and eager for the breathing room of the Pacific Northwest.

She came over to him, pulling him back from the windows, and led him to one of the side chairs.

"What are you doing?"

"Keeping you out of harm's way. That's my job."

"I'm pretty sure a sniper isn't something we have to worry about."

"Most people are pretty sure of that until they're dead. Better to be safe than sorry."

"Is that your mantra?" he asked.

That gray gaze of hers dropped and she shook her head. "No, that's not my mantra. But it's a good one for a man whose life has been threatened. Do you have any idea who could be behind the threats?"

He always played his cards close to his chest. This investigation was no different. If Sam hadn't relayed the information he'd already given to Charity, then neither would Daniel.

"No clue. I'm just a guy trying to run his business."

"Give me a break. You're one of the most powerful men in the import business."

"Yeah, there is that. But otherwise I'm just like everyone else."

"Most people who are being threatened have an idea why."

"I've discussed my thoughts with your boss."

She narrowed her gaze and he had the first glimpse of the woman he'd read about on paper. "Very well. When are we leaving?"

"In an hour. I have one last meeting in a few minutes."

"I'm going to check out the suite. How confident are you that your security team can protect you?"

"I hired you, didn't I?"

"You don't give much away, do you?"

"It doesn't pay in my business."

"Well, I'm your new best friend if you want to stay alive, so consider sharing with me," she said.

"Honey—"

"Please don't call me that. You may address me as Ms. Keone or Charity."

"Charity, then, I'm not the sharing type," he said. She might play at being tough as nails, but he was damned sure he would have to protect her if they got into any trouble.

What the hell was Sam Liberty doing hiring a woman like her?

"Wait here," he said, turning his back on her. He sent a message via his BlackBerry to Sam Liberty.

I need a bodyguard, not a distraction. Please send a replacement ASAP.

There was a rap on the door and he moved to open it. But Charity got there first, stopping the door from opening all the way, using her body to shield the room.

"How can I help you?" she asked.

"I need to speak to Mr. Williams," Alonzo said.

"What's your name?"

"Alonzo MacAfee. Tobias Jenner is here to see Mr. Williams."

Daniel walked over to Charity and tried to scoot past her. She stopped him with a hand on his arm.

"Mr. Williams, I need to secure the room before you enter it."

She definitely was going through all the motions of what he thought a bodyguard should. His BlackBerry twittered and he glanced at the message from Sam.

Keone is the best I know.

"I'm not going to need a bodyguard."

"Alonzo," Charity said, "please give us a moment. Have you searched Mr. Jenner?"

"Yes, ma'am. And this room is secure."

She nodded at Alonzo and then closed the door, leaning back against it. She crossed her arms over her chest.

"Why don't you need a bodyguard? Has the threat to you passed?"

"No, but I think I can handle this myself. In fact, I have from the beginning."

"Give me twenty-four hours to change your mind."

"Why?"

"I don't want to see you make a stupid mistake because you don't think I can do my job."

He refused to lie to her. "You're right—I don't believe you are capable of protecting me. I think you're probably really great at protecting celebrities on the red carpet because you blend in with the Hollywood crowd, but in my line of work, on this assignment, you're out of your league."

"What will it take to change your mind?" she asked.

"You can't," he said.

"Let me contact Sam."

She turned on her heel and left the main room of the suite and went to the little alcove just inside the main doorway.

He watched her go, wishing he was at a different point in his life where he could have indulged himself by keeping her around as his bodyguard.

Chapter Two

If you bring forth what is within you, what you bring forth will save you.

—Gospel of Thomas

Charity knew it was going to take more than divine scripture to save Daniel. He was stubborn and too sure of himself. She wasn't sure why she was surprised that Daniel didn't want her as his bodyguard. It wasn't the first time.

"Please contact your boss."

She smiled tightly at him and turned away, pulling her BlackBerry from her pocket.

<Charity>: DW wants me to leave him unguarded.

<Sam>: Give me a few minutes and I'll talk to him. We are still on the job.

<Charity>: I'll stay. But he's resistant to safety measures.

<Sam>: I have faith in you.

<Charity>: Thanks.

"Sam will be contacting you shortly. I can't leave until he pulls me off the job. Until then we'll operate with me as bodyguard."

"I don't have time to wait; I'm expecting a colleague for a meeting in a few minutes. In fact, you've left him standing in the hall."

He glanced down at his watch, clearly dismissing her from his mind. She shook her head and walked the perimeter of the room. The suite was spacious and well appointed, the main room divided into two different areas.

A loveseat and two wingback chairs were placed around a cherry wood coffee table. A dining room table with six chairs sat closer to the window. There was a desk in one corner near the window with a laptop computer set up on it.

"I'm going to be in a meeting."

"Who is the meeting with?"

"Tobias Jenner—he's in charge of my East Coast operation."

"Regular spelling on both names?" she asked, her thumbs moving over the keyboard on her BlackBerry.

"Yes. He's worked with me for over fifteen years. I don't think he's blackmailing me."

As soon as he affirmed the spelling she sent the name to Anna with a request for more info. Anna could find all the details on anyone in less than five minutes. She was pure magic with her computer.

"Blackmail is a crime of passion. This is someone who knows you."

"Tobias isn't the blackmailer."

She noticed he didn't say the blackmailer was a stranger. She tucked that away for later examination. She also noted the missing fingertip on his right hand. She wanted to know more about it and made a mental note to investigate. "You sound confident."

"I am."

"I'm not. I can't guard you unless I have all the information available."

He tipped his head to the side, studying her. She fought to stand still and appear as he wanted to see her, but she realized she'd just let him see a chink in her armor. Just let him glimpse something that wasn't part of her super-model image.

He walked closer to her and she stood her ground. She backed down for no one. Pride was one of her greatest strengths—and her biggest weakness. It was why she suspected things hadn't worked out with Perry. Ah, hell, she wasn't going to get into that right now.

"Do you trust Alonzo?" she asked.

"As much as I trust anyone," he said.

"You're not Confucius, so stop talking in riddles. This room is secure as long as you stay away from the window. I'll check out this Mr. Jenner and then escort him in here."

"You're not in charge," he said. "And I've got it all over Confucius."

"So says you, and until Sam pulls me off the job, I am in charge."

He crossed the room like he owned it, which she guessed he sort of did. His stride was long and his body language aggressive. He didn't stop until barely an inch separated them. His aftershave was outdoorsy and spicy and she tried to pretend she didn't like it, but lying went against the grain. Even white lies to herself.

She wished she could say that meeting him in person had made him seem less attractive. In person he exuded an animal magnetism that made her very aware of her femininity and angry that he didn't want her on the job, because she wanted to be with him. Not necessarily to work.

He put both hands on the door on either side of her head and leaned in. "I don't take orders."

"You give them?" she asked, trying to keep her wits about her. He was a distraction that she didn't need. The sheer physicality of him was so different from Perry's urbane smoothness. Daniel was raw, masculine—delicious, she thought. She put her hand on his sternum and pushed—he didn't budge. She could force the issue but she didn't, wanting to see how this would play out.

Instead he leaned closer, sinking his lower body against hers. "If you want to stay with me, alternative arrangements can be made."

"That's sexual harassment," she said.

His left hand caressed the side of her face, following the line of her neck to the base, where he rested his thumb over her pulse.

"Only if I said you could have the job if you sleep with me. I'm saying don't work for me but be my lover."

"I'm not really into being a rich man's plaything."

"Why not?"

"Because I have to look at myself in the mirror every morning," she said, bringing her hand up to capture his wrist. She did the same thing with his right hand, fingering the nub of his missing finger before drawing both wrists down to waist level.

"You like to be in control," he said, glancing at his wrists bound in her fists.

"Yes, I do," she said, moving her right foot and widening her stance. The only way Daniel was going to take her seriously was if she proved she was more than a pretty face. And the aikido move she had in mind should do the job nicely.

She pulled her left foot inward and brought her right arm across his chest, keeping her left arm fully extended forward, forcing Daniel to bend backward as her arm came down across his neck. She twisted her hips, following the movement through, throwing Daniel off balance and stepping away from him.

Daniel caught her wrists as she tried to step away, pinning her arms to her sides and stepping in close behind her. "I didn't realize you were familiar with aikido."

"Are you?" she asked.

He moved his right arm above his head, dragging her arm up with his, pulling her off balance. He wrapped an arm around her waist.

"Yes," he said. The easy way he held her told her that in one-on-one combat he could hold his own.

"Is this why you don't want a bodyguard?" she asked.

He swiveled his hips and she felt his erection nudge the small of her back. "No, this is."

"You're attracted to me," she said, so very tired of having men be turned on by her looks and not her skills or her brain.

"That's an understatement."

"You don't even know me," she said, bringing both of her hands to the arm around his waist and trying to subtly move her stance so that she'd be able to gain the advantage and throw him over her shoulder.

"I'm not going to let you gain the advantage here," he said, moving his stance so that they were back to where they'd been before.

She had a few other moves that she could use but they were down and dirty street fighting and would really hurt Daniel. Something she was oddly reluctant to do.

"I'd love to really spar with you," she said.

He laughed. "I think I'd like that, too. The next time I'm in D.C. I'll call you."

"So you still want me out?"

He dropped her arms and stepped away from her. "Yes. I think you'll prove to be more of a hindrance than a bodyguard."

"That's insulting," she said.

"I don't mean it to be," he said.

"Then how should I have taken it?"

He shrugged and straightened his suit coat. "Just that I want you and right now that could be a huge disadvantage for both of us."

"I've been in this business long enough to keep personal feelings out of the equation," she said, not sure what he was getting at.

He closed the distance between them again, cupping her jaw and tipping her head back. His mouth came down on hers, not hard like she'd been expecting, but so softly that she melted. He brushed his lips over hers repeatedly until she wanted to relax her guard and sink into him. To have his big, strong arms come around her. That freaked her out big-time because she wasn't usually distracted by men. Not even Senator Perry Jones, whom she'd thought she'd marry.

Daniel hadn't gotten to where he was in life by not going after what he wanted. And he wanted Charity Keone. He'd experienced lust before—hell, he was thirty-eight years old. He'd thought he was past the point where lust at first sight was an issue, but he was glad to be proved wrong.

Instinctively he'd known that forcing her to his will wasn't the way to get the kiss he wanted from her. And since they were going to part ways shortly, he saw no reason to deny himself a kiss. God, her mouth was so lush and full, it distracted him almost as much as her curvy body and her aikido moves. He was the first to admit he was drawn to strength.

There was something about Charity that spoke to him on more than one level. Any other woman he'd made a pass at would probably have accepted him for various reasons. He knew his money drew some of them, his strength others, and a few others sensed the dangerous quality that had saved him during his years on the street and were drawn to that.

But with Charity he sensed she was drawn to him in spite of all those things.

She encircled his neck with her hands and he tensed, not sure if she was going to caress him or crush him. The uncertainty was as much of a turn-on as her made-for-sin body.

The rapping on the door had him drawing away from her with a few soft, last-minute kisses. She shook her head. "You're very lucky, you're a good kisser."

"Is that what saved me?"

"This time," she said, palming a Sig Sauer from the holster under her arm and motioning for him to stay where he was.

"I'm pretty sure it's Alonzo," he said dryly. "Or maybe even Tobias."

"Pretty sure is a good way to end up dead. You have to know with absolute certainty who your enemy is, Mr. Williams."

"I think we are way past the point of formality."

"You're not as smart as you think you are, Mr. Williams."

He bit back a chuckle, thinking he might have been too hasty in telling Sam to send Charity packing. There was a real zest for life in the way she talked and moved.

She put one hand on the door and then opened it, keeping her gun in easy position for firing at a target.

"I think I'm expected," Tobias said. "You can put the gun away."

She didn't put the gun away—instead she pulled Tobias through the door. "Keep your hands where I can see them."

Tobias did as he was ordered and Charity quickly and efficiently searched the other man. Her total concentration and skill were a turn-on, Daniel thought. Her confidence showed through as she went about her job.

The woman he'd glimpsed when he'd kissed her a few minutes ago was gone. He wondered, as he watched the ultra-efficient bodyguard, which one was real.

Her BlackBerry twittered, but she didn't reach for the instrument.

"You may put your hands down now, but stay where you are."

"Is she new?" Tobias asked.

"No, I'm temporary," she said.

She put her gun away and picked up the BlackBerry. She read quickly, her eyes moving over the screen, and then nodded.

"I'll be right outside, Mr. Williams, until I hear from Sam."

Daniel watched her leave and turned his attention to business. Charity was a distraction—the last thing he needed right now. Too bad his body didn't agree.

"Temporary?" Tobias asked as soon as the door shut behind her. "I can make room for her on my staff."

Daniel shook his head. He knew that Tobias wouldn't be able to handle a woman like Charity. She was more than met the eye, and his colleague was looking at the super-model and thinking she'd make a nice ornament. The first time she showed him her teeth, Tobias would probably run for the hills.

"What is the problem with Customs?" Daniel said, forcing the subject to business.

"I can't get anyone from the office to call us back. We're in quarantine and they won't lift it."

"We don't even carry anything that could be disease-bearing. I'll make a few calls and see what I can do."

"I've been on the phone for two days."

This kind of thing was a nuisance and Daniel could totally see Sekijima's hand in this. It would be just like his old friend to bribe someone to make Daniel's life harder.

"Let me give it a try. Anything else?"

"Not unless you will authorize my hiring your temporary employee."

"Not going to happen."

"Are you interested in her?" Tobias asked.

"She is a very beautiful woman."

Tobias stood up and Daniel watched the other man leave. He put in two calls to friends he had in Customs. And had to leave messages both times.

He walked over to the window, ignoring Charity's rule to stay away. He wanted Sekijima to see him. To know that Daniel wasn't afraid of him. The Japanese understood "face." Hell, Daniel had learned about it from Sekijima. His old friend was coming back for his blood, and Daniel could understand that but he was tired of waiting.

Tired of the attacks on those around him. He knew they were the opening volley in a deadly game that Sekijima was playing. Daniel was ready for the waiting to stop. Once Charity was out of the picture and he was back in Seattle, he was going to leave the corporate CEO behind and go after Sekijima in the only way the other man would understand. He rubbed his right shoulder where the tail of his dragon tattoo rested. Sekijima might be the Oyabun of the Yakuza but Daniel had once been his Gashira Hosa—second in command—and Daniel had learned all of his boss's secrets.

When Charity closed the door quietly behind her and took a moment to scan the hallway, she noticed that Alonzo was on the phone and not really very alert. The job, always her saving grace, gave her the impetus she needed not to think about what had happened with Daniel.

Alonzo MacAfee was a tall black man with intense eyes and the kind of muscles that came from working out in a gym a lot of hours every day. He glanced up as she entered the hallway and then went back to lounging against the wall. He had his Bluetooth phone activated and she could tell he was in conversation. When the conversation continued for more than a few minutes, she grew concerned that there could be a threat to Daniel.

She tapped him on the arm. "Alonzo? Is there a security matter that I need to be made aware of?"

He hit the mute button and shook his head. "I'm talking to my girl."

"Hang up the phone right now."

"I don't work for you."

"No, but you do work for Mr. Williams. His security is your number one priority."

He patted his shoulder holster. "I've got my eye on the hall and my gun. We're good."

"I'm not going to ask you again."

She didn't back down and neither did Alonzo, who simply glared at her. But after a minute he told his girl he'd call her later.

"Now we need to discuss security for getting Mr. Williams from the hotel to the airport."

"His car has bulletproof windows and I'll be at his side the entire time," Alonzo said. He flexed his muscles under the custom-made suit. "Trust me—no one gets through me."

"A bullet could."

"Not many snipers gunning for Mr. Williams."

"Perhaps in the past. What have you done to upgrade security measures since the attack on his domestic staff?"

"Why do you care, pretty girl?"

She let the "pretty girl" comment pass. "Because I was hired to be his bodyguard, which tells me someone thought you needed reinforcements."

Alonzo bristled and then ran down the security measures he'd put in place. They were extensive, and aside from the conversation with his girlfriend, she had to say he seemed to be very competent.

"I'd like to make sure that the kitchen and cargo elevator are secure. We'll take him down that way," Charity said.

"Why? All the incidents have taken place in Seattle."

She shook her head. She'd expected better from this man who was the head of Daniel's security. "Precisely. Whoever is threatening him will expect our guard to be lax here."

"Granted. I'll check the kitchen and back hallway," Alonzo said.

"Good. Call me when the area is secure," she said, giving him her cell number.

Alonzo walked away and Charity remained hyper-alert watching the hallway. A few minutes later, Tobias emerged from the room. He gave her the kind of flirty smile she was used to. She returned it but declined his invitation for drinks later.

She got a text-message from Sam informing her she was off the job once they reached the airport. She had mixed feelings about the ending of the assignment. There had been something about Daniel . . . but that wasn't what she should be focused on. And she refused to regret that their one brief kiss would be all there would ever be between them.

Chapter Three

Every noble work is, at first, impossible.
                              —Thomas Carlyle

Charity kept Ralph Waldo Emerson's admonition in the front of her mind as Daniel emerged from his suite. But it was hard. Beyond the façade of the businessman in control of his environment, she saw the signs of strain. Stress no doubt worsened by having your life threatened.

"Where's Alonzo?"

"I sent him downstairs to secure the area."

"Didn't Sam tell you that I don't need you anymore?" he asked, striding down the hall toward the guest elevators.

"We'll part company once you're on the jet. We're not going down through the lobby."

"Why not?"

"Because someone has threatened your life."

He paused. "I hired you because I want to set myself up as bait. Didn't Sam tell you that?"

"You fired me so you can do that once I'm gone."

He shook his head.

"Daniel—"

"I thought you'd never say my name."

She shook her head. "You have to have a plan before you act like bait. Otherwise . . . you'll end up dead."

He didn't say anything else—they were too exposed in the

hallway. She kept alert, watching the rooms, trying to see around the curve to their left and watching the elevators.

"We can talk about your plan in the car. Even though you no longer require a bodyguard, we can help you design—"

"I'm sick of waiting. It puts all the power in the hands of my blackmailer."

She took his arm and drew him down the hall to the maintenance hallway. It was empty and she felt slightly less exposed here.

"I can understand that. Who is the blackmailer?"

"Someone from my past."

"Do you have the name?" she asked.

"It could be any number of people," he said.

She sensed he wasn't telling the truth, but it was his life and she wasn't going to be on the job in a few hours. "Honesty could be the key to staying alive."

"I'm thirty-eight, Charity. I think I know a thing or two about staying alive."

"Maybe in the corporate world."

"In any world," he said.

She wondered what he meant by that but tried to stay focused on the job and not on personal stuff. And that type of question would definitely be personal.

"What does the blackmailer want?"

"Two of my ships to import cargo."

"What kind of cargo?" she asked, leading him down the hall to the freight elevator. She keyed Alonzo's number into her BlackBerry. "Just a minute."

"MacAfee."

"It's Charity—is the kitchen secure?"

"Yes."

"We're coming down."

She turned back to Daniel. He was watching her in a very masculine way that she knew had nothing to do with the job at hand. It was a man-woman kind of stare that she should have been used to, but the intensity in Daniel was different from the way other men looked at her.

"So what kind of cargo?" she asked.

"The illegal kind."

He was being elusive and she guessed if she'd been approached to do something illegal she'd do the same. But it made her wonder. "Why you?"

"I told you it has something to do with my past. Why are we going down the back way?"

"So that anyone who knows you are leaving today won't realize you've left."

"That makes sense, but won't my enemies be watching all entrances?"

Did he think she was incompetent? "Of course they will be. But the kitchen area has fewer people than a lobby full of guests and staff. Alonzo's already cleared the area and we'll walk straight out to your car."

"You've thought of everything," he said. "But my enemies will, too."

He did think she couldn't handle the job. "I assure you, Daniel, I'm on top of this."

"I believe you," he said.

But she wondered if he really did. "Was your driver hired from the same company as the pilot for your private jet?"

"Yes, why?"

"No reason. Anna is running a check on the company and so far hasn't come up with any red flags."

"Who's Anna?"

"The computer expert on the team. She's in charge of technology and information."

"How many are on your team?"

"There are three of us."

"All women?"

"Yes, why? Does that bother you?" she asked. Sam didn't say much but she knew some of their clients thought that an all-female team couldn't handle the jobs they took on. The fact that those clients were soon proved wrong always made Charity feel good.

"No. It's every man's fantasy to have a gorgeous woman guarding his body."

"Stop it, Daniel."

"Stop what?"

"The sexist flirting."

"Why? We're not working together."

"It's insulting, that's why. We are working together until I get you safely to the jet."

"This is a walk-in-the-park assignment for you."

She shook her head. "Assumptions like that lead to mistakes."

"And you don't make mistakes."

"I'm human so of course I'm not perfect, but I do try to plan for any eventuality."

The freight elevator doors closed and she depressed the down button. The floor of the elevator was dirty. It had doors that opened on either side, and she focused on positioning herself for a clear view at either entrance.

She didn't like the setup because she wasn't confident about Alonzo or his abilities. She wanted Justine and Anna close by so she knew they had her back like they always did. But instead she had to use backup that had been . . .

Daniel's cologne smelled so good, she thought. Then cursed. What the hell was she thinking? She had to keep her mind on the job. Getting him out of this building and onto his jet. Afterwards she could dwell on how delicious he smelled.

"Have you planned for this?" Daniel asked, stepping closer to her and lowering his head.

She sidestepped out of his way. "Not now, Daniel."

"Yes, now," he said. "As soon as I get on that plane we'll never see each other again. And so far you're the only good thing to come out of this blackmail mess."

She smiled up at him. "You do have a certain charm."

He lowered his head again. Determined to prove to himself that she wasn't any different from the other beautiful women he'd been involved with over the course of his life. To prove to himself that he'd just imagined that spark of something different.

Her skin was like porcelain—exquisite, even in the harsh light of the maintenance elevator. Her lips were a deep red and he realized she'd taken time to reapply her lipstick. What bodyguard thought of doing that?

She gave him a quick kiss on his cheek and stepped to the side. "But not enough. If we weren't working together . . ."

"I think I already took care of that."

"Yes, you did. Next time you're in D.C., call me."

"Charity," he said, running his hand down the center of her back. She shivered and turned her head to the side so all he could see was the fall of her blond hair.

"Don't."

She stepped away from him and took two deep breaths, and the vivacious woman he'd seen just a second ago was gone. She was all icy Amazon now, the walls firmly in place as they reached the lowest floor.

The door to their left opened and she stepped in front of him. He hated the fact that she was using her body to shield him. He reached for her arm, drew her to a halt.

"We go together."

"I'm your bodyguard," she said.

He just held fast and refused to let go. Alonzo was a bodyguard, and Daniel had absolutely no problem letting him do his job. But Charity? Hell, no. He wasn't letting her be the target instead of him. Not that he thought Sekijima would attack here, though his usual M.O. was to strike quickly and leave no one alive. The fact that Mildred was only in the I.C.U. and not the morgue had made Daniel realize that Sekijima was out for his blood.

She twisted her arm in his grip but he held strong. "This is utterly ridiculous."

"I agree."

"I'm still on the job here."

"What kind of man lets a woman take a bullet for him?" he asked.

"I thought you were convinced there was no threat here."

"Your diligence changed my mind."

She drew him out of the pathway in the kitchen. The busboys, dishwashers, and sous chefs all went about their business, each of them working at their own stations. The smell of garlic cooking in olive oil was pungent and evocative.

"Don't think of me as a woman," she said.

"Impossible."

She tilted her head to the side, staring at him. "All my other clients have had no problem letting me do my job. I need you to do that as well, Daniel."

"I can't get the feel of you in my arms out of my mind."

She shook her head. "I can make you forget it."

"Are you threatening me?" he asked, intrigued.

She shrugged but didn't relax her vigilance. It was amazing, he thought. Seeing her like this, he understood why she had the reputation she did. He admired her for her professionalism. But Sekijima would see that same determination and spirit and use it to break her.

Did that matter to him? She was little more than a stranger. Yet at the same time she was more than a stranger. More than a beautiful face.

"Answer me."

"What do you want me to say? You're a very good-looking man, as I'm sure you know, but to me you are still a client, someone I'm committed to protecting. If I have to use force to do that, then I will."

"I'm not talking about the superficial—didn't you feel the attraction between us?"

"If I say no, are you going to try more of your aikido on me?"

"Would it work?"

She cracked a smile. "No. Let's go to your car to discuss this further. I don't like stopping here in the open."

He nodded. She positioned herself in front of him and to the left. But he was left-handed and knew he needed that side clear. He pulled her to his right side.

She raised one eyebrow at him in question.

"I'm left-handed."

She accepted his explanation and pulled on a pair of dark sunglasses. He did the same. It was the middle of the day and the bright sunlight would momentarily blind them otherwise.

He felt a moment of something that he refused to acknowledge. A moment of teamwork and sharing, a sense of rightness at having this woman by his side in a dangerous situation. But he knew he was a loner.

That he had secrets she'd want to uncover if he let her stay on in her role as a bodyguard. Secrets that he knew would endanger her and lead to her death.

They approached the exit and she stopped one more time. "Don't try to be the hero here, Daniel. Let me do my job."

"I've never been the hero," he said, knowing that was more true than he hoped she'd ever know.

"Just stay behind me and let me do my job."

He nodded because he had the feeling she'd stand there all day until he agreed. But he'd never let anyone take a hit for him, even when he'd been an eighty-pound street punk, getting the crap kicked out of him nightly. It just wasn't in his nature to let someone else take his place.

Especially not a woman like Charity.

They stepped outside together. She directed them to the left of the alleyway where he saw the Rolls Royce sedan he'd rented. Alonzo stood next to the rear door and his driver was already behind the wheel.

Alonzo had never shown such diligence before, and Daniel suspected that Charity had given him a lecture similar to the one he'd gotten. He admired her work ethic and dedication to the job. Too bad he couldn't quit admiring her other assets.

But c'est la vie. And his was very complicated right now. Alonzo opened the door as they approached, and from the corner of his eye he saw some movement at the lip of the alley.

Time slowed as he saw Alonzo turn toward the woman walking toward them. A split second later she pulled a handgun from under her raincoat and fired at point-blank range.

Chapter Four

True self is the part of us that does not change when circumstances do.

—Mason Cooley

Charity welcomed the chance to embrace her true self as she shoved Daniel to the side and brought up her weapon. She fired off one round and realized that her angle was wrong. She'd brushed her target's thigh, but that was all.

The target fired back, hitting Alonzo, and she stepped in front of Daniel to protect him with her body if need be. She wore a Kevlar vest, so she wasn't too worried about getting hit. And she knew she could get her target if she was in the right position.

But the target spun on her heel and took off. She drew Daniel to his feet, but he jerked his arm out of her grasp and took off at a dead run after his assailant.

"Dammit, Daniel!"

But he said nothing, just ran flat-out and with more speed than she'd expected from an executive. She took one moment to yell at Daniel's driver to call 911 for Alonzo, then followed Daniel.

They'd disappeared around the front of the building toward the hotel entrance. She caught a brief glimpse of the target weaving through the crowd. Charity paused for a moment to take in the entire situation and assess the best way to catch the woman who'd tried to kill her client.

She analyzed the paths through the crowd and the cars and then crossed the street. There was a lot less foot traffic on that side. She lengthened her gait and dug in, running flat-out. She kept Daniel in her sights as well as the target.

She hit a button on her belt, alerting her team that she needed them. She finally got ahead of her target, and crossed the street again. The target slowed, realizing she was trapped between her and Daniel. But then she dashed out into the street, nearly missing being hit by a city bus.

Charity cursed and took off after her. The bus had slowed traffic, and Charity was able to get to the other side just in time to see her target climb onto the back of a Harley-Davidson and drive away.

She memorized the license plate and turned around to confront Daniel as he came up behind her.

"What the hell were you doing?" she asked, while breathing heavily.

"I wanted to question her," Daniel said, his breath just as heavy as hers.

"I can't protect you if you're going to do stupid things like that."

"My plan isn't to be protected. It's to find the person threatening me and confront them."

"Ah, so you're hoping to end up dead?"

"I almost had her."

"I know. I didn't think she'd bolt into traffic. Why didn't I think of that?"

He shrugged. And she realized now wasn't the time to analyze what had gone wrong. Daniel was vulnerable out on the street. He started walking back toward his car and she hurried to keep up with him. He was tense and angry but something else was going on with him as well.

"You okay?"

"Why wouldn't I be?"

"Someone just tried to kill you."

"It's not the first time."

"What do you mean?"

"Just that I've ruffled feathers before. Was Alonzo okay?"

"I didn't stop to check. I asked the driver to call 911."

"Why didn't you stop? I was clearly in pursuit."

"Because my job is to protect you, not Alonzo. And why didn't you stay put?"

"That's not in my programming."

He fascinated her, she thought. He was complex, and she had the feeling that he had as many different layers as she did. That he was used to letting people see what they wanted to see, something she was very familiar with.

They approached the car and found an ambulance and the cops waiting for them. Justine was already working the crime scene, talking to witnesses.

The cops immediately drew Daniel aside and started questioning him. But he wouldn't cooperate until he knew that Alonzo was being taken care of.

She watched him talking to the EMTs and realized that loyalty was important to him. That his people were important to him.

"You're staring," Justine said, coming up behind her.

"I'm not staring; I'm keeping an eye on him. This area isn't too secure."

"I know. He doesn't act like a man who just had his life threatened."

"He's arrogant."

"And pissed off," Justine said.

"He's not what I expected."

"What'd you expect? Someone like Senator Perry?"

"I guess. He's not our normal client. There's more going on here than just blackmail."

"Ya think? Did the bullet exchange change your mind?"

Charity punched her friend in the arm. "You're being annoying."

"That's part of my appeal."

"Maybe that's why you're always alone."

"No, that's not the reason. Ready to walk me through what happened? Anna's inside talking to the staff, trying to get a bead on whether anyone saw the sniper earlier."

"That's good," she said. "Do you have a description?"

"Yes, Alonzo gave us a fairly good one."

"Ms. Keone?"

"Yes?"

"I'm Officer Blane Ketting—I'd like to take your statement now."

"I need to make sure that Mr. Williams is in a secure area before I talk to you."

"I'll go find an office inside that we can use," Justine said, walking away.

She noticed that Officer Ketting watched her friend go. Justine never realized her appeal to the opposite sex . . . well, that wasn't necessarily true. Justine didn't like her appeal to the opposite sex.

"That's fine. We're securing this area. Do you want to go back to the station?"

"I'd rather not. Can you give Justine five minutes to find us a place?"

She knew that Sam would already have contacted the police department, using his contacts to alert them to what was going on. The officer backed off and she went over to Daniel.

Daniel watched the ambulance pull away with another one of his people in it. Another one of his people had been injured in this war that Sekijima had started. And it could be nothing else. Sekijima was coming after him old-school style, striking at his family and weakening him.

He needed to kick something or strangle someone—preferably that bitch who had tried to kill him. He felt a soft touch on his shoulder and turned around with a glare.

Charity didn't back off but he saw her guard come up. "What is it?"

"Nothing." He fucking wasn't going to tell her that he was angry because this was twice that he'd been struck in his own house, so to speak. He wasn't about to start talking because he knew that expletives and impotent rage weren't meant to be expressed vocally. They needed to be channeled into a single focus. And now she was in danger. He knew the assassin that Sekijima had sent had gotten a good look at Charity.

Hell, she was impossible to miss with her blond hair and knockout body, but more than that, the other woman would have recognized the trained fighter that Charity was. She'd almost caught the assassin and that would be the first thing that Sekijima would be told about Charity.

He was going to fucking find Sekijima and ring his goddamned neck. But first he had to find a way to protect her. He figured he'd have to keep her with him if he was going to keep her safe.

"Take a deep breath, Daniel."

"Why?" he asked, his mind racing over the possibilities.

"Because you look like you're about to do something crazy, and the cops are still here."

"Fuck that. I'm not worried about the cops." And he wasn't. He could handle them if he had to. He'd made friends in high places since leaving the streets.

She drew him away from the cops, processing the scene and looking for evidence. He noticed almost absently that she still protected him with her body and kept the wall at his back. She was really top-notch at what she did.

"I'm sorry I was crass," he said.

"Don't be. I want to curse, too."

Without a second thought, he drew her to him and claimed the kiss he'd wanted in the elevator. He knew it was a piss-poor decision but he needed to taste her. Wanted to feel her tongue moving against his. He groaned in the back of his throat as her hands came up around his neck. She arched into him and then slowly drew back.

He let her go because he knew he had to. But that one taste wasn't nearly enough to satisfy him. He wanted more of this woman. And now he'd endangered her life.

"Daniel," she said. Just his name falling from her lips, and he knew he wanted to hear it again. Hear it when they were both naked and he was buried hilt-deep in her silky body.

"I can't believe that bitch got away," he said, forcing his mind off the images of Charity in his arms.

"We'll find her. I got the tag and Anna's already running the plates."

"It'll be a dead end."

"Even dead ends have clues," she said.

Her voice was firm and he felt her resolve. "I'm firing you, remember? Why do you care?"

"It's what I do. It's what we do for all of our clients," she said.

"Is that all I am to you? Another client?"

"We hardly know each other."

"I guess that's my answer."

"What do you want me to say, Daniel? You intrigue me, but this isn't going anywhere. Right now you're looking for a place to channel your rage."

He hated how clearly she saw him. So many people were content just to see the surface man. The quasi-civilized façade he presented to the world. But not Charity. He suspected that was because she had a mask of her own.

But he didn't really care why. He didn't like anyone to see the parts of himself he hid. And he knew just the way to drive her away. And he needed to drive her away. He needed her angry and walking out of his life. Because a split second before she'd shoved him to the ground, he realized that she'd take a bullet for him.

"I am," he said. "Could I tempt you back up to my room? I think an hour in bed with you—"

"Don't. I'm not going to let you use sexist comments to drive me away."

"I don't have to; you are off the job anyway."

"Not until I see you safely to your jet."

"Mr. Williams? Ms. Keone? We really need your statements."

Daniel walked away from Charity and didn't look back. He followed the officer into the hotel and through the lobby. He was hyper-aware of everything going on around him. He searched the faces in the crowd—knowing Sekijima well enough to know that he'd have people planted there. People in place in case his assassin failed.

But the faces were all unremarkable. Some tourists, some businessmen, no one who stood out. Which was exactly what he'd expect from Sekijima and his people. All the same, Daniel studied them and memorized the faces. Sekijima didn't have unlimited resources and Daniel knew from experience that Sekijima's inner circle would be small.

"Do you recognize anyone?" Charity asked under her breath as they moved through the lobby.

"Not yet."

"Do you know who's threatening you?" she asked.

Her insight made him realize that he was wasting an opportunity to use her talents. She saw him too clearly, and he didn't want her to know the real man he had buried beneath years of pretending to be wealthy and sophisticated. But he wouldn't mind using her special abilities to track down Sekijima and his killers.

He hurried his pace and glanced over his shoulder one last time before they entered the hallway behind the front desk. He glanced not at Charity but at the sea of faces.

One of these faces, Daniel would see again. And when he did, he'd act.

                              *   *   *

Charity couldn't get a handle on Daniel and gave up when he pointedly turned away from her in the office where the police were questioning them. Justine and Anna were already in there, Anna seated with her laptop up and running and Justine leaning over her shoulder.

This was just not her day, she thought. She walked over to her team and immediately felt a sense of peace steal over her. Justine didn't mention Daniel again or the fact that Charity had been watching him with more than just diligence on her mind.

"What have you found?" Charity asked.

"The cops found a spent casing and we think a bullet is lodged in MacAfee's body. We're hoping to get a ballistics match on that one," Anna said. "This is a rough composite sketch of the shooter. Does it match what you saw?"

Charity leaned down and studied the face on the screen. She closed her eyes for a second and recalled the details of the woman who'd tried to kill Daniel.

The face of the Asian woman was etched in Charity's mind and the next time she saw her, Charity wouldn't hesitate to take her out of the game. Self-anger wasn't productive but she was ticked off that she'd let this assassin slip through her fingers.

The computer program that Anna was using was state-of-the-art and had millions of facial features to choose from. "The eyes were a little further apart. And her bangs were swept completely off her forehead."

Anna made a few adjustments with her mouse and then leaned back. Charity checked it again, comparing the image in her mind with the one on the screen. "That's it. Daniel might be able to add more details."

"Daniel?" Anna asked.

"Our client. What did you find out about the driver and pilot that he's using?"

"The driver is with the cops now, talking to them about what he saw. The company he uses checks out and the personnel assigned to him have been working for them for over five years," Justine said. "I'm nearly as certain as I can be that they are legit and not a threat."

Justine never trusted anything or anyone all the way. Which was one of the things that made her such an asset to the team. Anna was the most trusting of the three of them. She tended to believe in people until she had proof that they weren't trustworthy. Charity, on the other hand, fell somewhere in the middle.

Was that why she was struggling with Daniel? He was one of those gray areas that she wanted to trust but her gut was screaming at her that he was hiding something.

Of course he was, she thought—he's being blackmailed.

"Charity?"

"Huh?"

"Do you want me to take over guard duty at the airport?"

She shook her head. "No. It's my job, I'll finish it. I would like you and Anna to get there before us, check the plane and make sure that everything is as it should be."

"I agree," Justine said. "Whoever is after Mr. Williams is serious about taking him out. Two strikes in two days."

"If they are so serious, why isn't he dead?" Charity asked out loud.

"I don't know," Anna said. "Maybe they just want him scared."

"Could be, or maybe his blackmailer is toying with him?" Justine suggested.

"I'm betting on the latter," Charity said. "Daniel plans to set himself up as bait."

"We're off the case after he gets on that plane," Justine said.

"I want to talk to Sam again, see if he can get us back on the case. Anna, did you find anything in your databases that Daniel won't have access to?"

"What are you thinking?" Justine asked.

"I want to prove to him that he needs us."

"We don't prove ourselves to anyone, Charity, and you know that. If he wants to play his game, then let him."

She couldn't let it go. She knew that Justine was right, but a part of her . . . just felt like she needed to stay with Daniel or he would die. And she didn't want to see him killed because of his own stubbornness.

"I'm going to call Sam."

"So be it. I'm going to get Mr. Williams to look at Anna's sketch and see if we can't get some more information out of him."

"Sam might say no," Charity said, realizing that Justine was already acting like they were going to get the go-ahead from Sam to stay on the case.

"Yeah, right. He never says no if we are determined to stay on a case," Anna said.

Charity left her friends and stepped outside the office. She speed-dialed Sam's secured number. Anna was right about Sam. He always backed them up, even when prudence said he shouldn't. But this wasn't a case of bad judgment.

"Yes, Charity?"

"I want to stay on the Williams job. I know he's dead set against working with a woman bodyguard, but I think he needs us."

"Actually, he's not. I just got a text message from him that he's changed his mind." As always, there were no noises in the background to betray where he was.

"Why?"

"He didn't say."

"Can you talk to him?"

"I intend to as soon as I'm finished in a meeting."

She wondered what Sam's real life was like. She knew that their team was just one of half a dozen he had in different locations all over the world.

"He's hiding something about his past," she said. "I'm not sure it's relevant to what's going on now, but it might be. He said that the blackmailer wants him to do something illegal. Why would they ask him?"

"I'm not sure that matters, Charity."

"It does to me," she said.

"Why is this important to you?"

She thought about it for a moment. Didn't want to lie to her boss or to herself. "It just is."

Sam said nothing, and in the silence she realized she was going to have to give him something more than those brief words.

"I have this feeling in my gut that I can save his life, but I can't unless I have all the information on him." she said.

"Very well. I'll see what I can do."

"Thanks, Sam."

"Don't thank me yet. Did Anna find anything in our databases on the assassin?"

"No, but you know how determined she is. If that woman is in any database in the world, Anna will find her."

"Yes, I know. I think that might work in our favor with Mr. Williams."

She hung up with Sam and went back into the office. She met Daniel's gaze across the room and something passed between them. She looked away first, uncomfortable as she realized that she wanted to stay on the job with Daniel for more than business.

Chapter Five

Arriving at one goal is the starting point to another.
—John Dewey

Charity was very aware that John Dewey wasn't infallible. She'd reached more than one goal to find a dead end. But with Daniel's acquiescence, she felt like it was a starting point.

"So you're going to Seattle with me."

"Yes, I am. Why'd you change your mind?"

"After seeing you in action I knew you could do the job," he said.

But the words felt like a lie. Like there was something more to his reason for changing his mind. She hadn't questioned it before because it had been what she'd wanted, but now she did.

They were in the Rolls, headed toward the executive airport. His attention had been on the passing cars and scenery. But she knew that he was still going over the attempt on his life.

She put her hand on his leg. "But you'd already seen me in action and hadn't changed your mind."

He put his hand over hers and turned toward her. There was fire in his silvery gaze and she felt . . . too much. Not at all what she'd expected, and she knew that was why she'd asked Sam to try again. She liked the unexpectedness of being with Daniel.

"I can't explain it further than that. Sam mentioned you'd called him as well. Were you going to ask him to talk to me again?"

She had never been tentative in her life. And she wasn't about to start now, but it would be so nice just to disappear into herself for a few moments. "Yes, I was."

"Why?"

"I didn't want to see you go."

"Personally?"

She made a noncommittal noise. She knew that she wanted him but it was more than lust. She also had that tingling in her gut that said she could save his life. She'd been saving lives for so long that she knew better than to ignore it.

"Come on, Charity, tell me your secrets," he said.

"Will you tell me yours?"

"Maybe."

"Maybe's not good enough."

"Then give me something to work with," he said.

"What?"

"Cop to what you're feeling," he said. He angled his body on the seat so he was facing her.

"I'm intrigued by you," she said, against her better judgment. Oh, who was she kidding? When it came to Daniel, she had no judgment. He made her react on every level.

He gave her a half-smile, running his misshapen index finger down the side of her face. He traced the line of her jaw and then feathered his thumb over her lips. She parted them and was tempted to bite him. Just to remind him she was still in charge.

But she didn't feel like she was in charge as he tipped her head back and leaned forward. She felt like she was under his spell. Very few men could get around her so easily . . . why was she letting him do this to her?

She put her hand on his face, felt the warmth of his body.

He moved his lips on hers and she tunneled her fingers into his hair, holding him still.

She thrust her tongue deep into his mouth and tasted everything that was Daniel. The warm masculinity and raw power, and she wanted more of it. She wanted this man that she sensed could be her equal on every level.

On every level.

She pulled back, knowing that she had things deep inside that she'd never shared with anyone. Things that didn't fit with her super-model looks or her near-genius IQ.

"What?"

"That was . . ."

"Perfect. The flight to Seattle will give us time to get to know one another better."

"Not intimately."

He shrugged. "Whatever you say."

"Don't, Daniel."

"Don't what?"

"Treat me like arm candy. I think I've already proven to you that I'm more than that."

He rubbed the bridge of his nose and dropped his hands from her.

"You have."

The silence spread between them as the miles flew past and they continued down the highway.

"You can't be more than a bodyguard to me."

"Why not?"

"Because my enemy is looking for weaknesses."

"I'm not a weakness. I'm one tough cookie."

"But still a cookie," he said, almost under his breath.

"I didn't mean it that way. I've held my own under extreme circumstances."

"You've never faced an enemy like this one before."

"Tell me what we're facing."

"I told you—someone from my past."

He was hiding something from her. What?

"Tell me more. You can trust me."

"It's not you that I don't trust, Charity."

"Who, then?"

"Everyone. I learned the hard way to rely only on myself."

"I'm self-reliant, too," she said. "But really good to have at your side."

"I've hired you to guard my back."

"You are so stubborn."

He just shrugged. His cell phone rang and he took the call. She realized she was watching him and listening to the deep cadence of his voice when he arched one eyebrow at her. God, she wasn't falling for him . . .

She palmed her BlackBerry from her pocket and sent a quick message to Anna, asking for an update on Daniel's background.

She got an immediate response that said—*still searching.* Still searching through his past. She had a suspicion they weren't going to find anything relevant. Daniel had the look of a man who knew how to keep his secrets hidden. She was going to have to get him to talk, and she was oddly reluctant to use her femininity to do it. She felt like they'd moved beyond that kind of manipulation.

She was about to put the BlackBerry away when a message popped up from Justine telling her to delay getting to the airport. She wanted more time to go over the plane.

"Henry, don't go directly to the airport," she said.

"Why not?" Daniel asked. "Stay on course, Henry."

"Yes, sir," Henry said.

"They aren't finished vetting the plane. Daniel, it's not safe until we know what we are dealing with there."

"What do you suggest? Ride around the city?"

She rolled her eyes at him. "Of course not. Do you mind if

we stop by my place so I can pack a bag for the trip to Seattle?"

He arched one eyebrow at her. "I don't mind. Give Henry your address."

She leaned forward, giving the chauffeur the information he needed. Bringing Daniel to her private space might not be the best idea, but she knew her house was secure and she could protect him there from any threat.

Daniel was surprised when the Rolls stopped in front of a gated house just outside of the metro D.C. area. Charity leaned out the window and keyed a code that opened the gate. Henry pulled through and Charity asked him to wait until the gate closed before continuing up the drive.

She was cautious and alert until the gates closed and they started up the driveway. Her house was large—too large for one person, but he was getting the impression that security was important to her. Maybe he could convince her to stay at her home until the threat from Sekijima passed. Then she'd be out of harm's way and he wouldn't have to take her to Seattle with him.

"Henry, you can wait in the portico around the side there. There's a gas pump if we need to refuel as well as a kitchen area if you're hungry."

Daniel exited the car. "How long will we be?"

"I'm not sure. I have to wait for Justine to give us the all-clear."

"I'm not used to just sitting around," he said.

"We can use this time to talk about a strategy," she said as Henry pulled away. She led the way up the stone stairs to her front door.

She keyed in a code and the door unlocked with an audible click. Daniel reached for the knob and held the door open for her. She smiled her thanks and entered the house.

She paused in the doorway as if reluctant to let him in. But then she walked inside and he followed her.

The foyer was exquisitely crafted with art glass. Not Tiffany but maybe Chihuly. The floor was a mosaic design that felt Japanese to him, a circular design of a man and a woman wrapped around each other in yin/yang pose. Around them were different elements—earth, fire, water, air.

Above them in the three-story-tall atrium was a huge glass installation that mirrored the colors on the floor. Especially when they stepped into the foyer and she opened a walnut panel door concealed in the wall.

"This is my command center," she said.

He followed her inside. One wall was lined with monitors, another wall with a floor-to-ceiling cabinet, and the last wall with computers. Not just one but three. There was a Liberty Investigations logo dancing on one of the screens, a picture of Charity and Justine and Anna on another screen, and a samurai on the last one.

"Is this where you plot to take over the world?" he asked, half joking.

"I could. But I prefer to use my powers for good and not evil."

She said it in jest but he knew that she was solidly on the law-abiding side. That was what made his attraction to her so impossible. He knew that nothing could come of it. Nothing other than a red-hot affair. Besides, his life was in danger and someone was trying to kill him. Not exactly the time to be thinking of getting involved with any woman.

But then, sensible had never been one of the qualities he aspired to. She went to the computer with the Liberty Investigations logo and sat down, her long fingers moving over the keyboard. He didn't read over her shoulder, but looked around the room. He opened the door to the cabinet and noticed that it was lined with weapons. Not just handguns but assault rifles and grenades. Fighting swords, aikido sticks, knives . . . every possible weapon known to man.

"Very impressive arsenal you have here."

"Thanks. I like to be prepared for anything. I still can't believe I let that assassin slip by me."

"Don't beat yourself up over it. Most people wouldn't risk getting hit by a bus."

She shrugged. She finished typing and turned to him. "Okay, so what are we up against? Sam said you wanted to set yourself up as bait—how do plan to do that?"

He didn't want to talk strategy with her. He wanted to see her house and uncover the secrets she held so close to her chest.

But she gave him a steely-eyed look and he knew she wasn't going to back down. He had no idea how much to tell her. His gut instinct was to keep her completely out of it. Like Charity, he intended to set up the situation in a way where he could control all the variables. And the only way to do that was to keep everyone off guard. To keep them dependent on him.

"I'm going to return to my home, dismiss my remaining staff, turn off my security system, arm myself, and wait."

She nodded. "Make your enemy come to you. Anna, Justine, and I can provide security at your place."

She turned back to the computer and opened up a file which showed an aerial view of his house on one of the San Juan Islands. "Are you thinking of this place or your high-rise apartment in Seattle?"

"The San Juan home," he said. "I don't want to risk anyone else's life. And I want to be away from the city where I can control who is on the property."

"Perfect. I think we have a schematic of the property somewhere . . ."

He leaned over her shoulder, looking at the screen. "There are two ways onto the island . . . the first is here at the boat dock and the second is the airfield."

"Do you have an alarm system set up to alert the main house when anyone lands or docks?"

"Of course. We can't use too many motion sensors because of the wildlife on the island."

"We can set up something when we get out there. I think I'm going to need the entire team to set this up. We should plan on taking a few days to get the island the way we want it."

"I'm not sure my enemy is going to just sit and wait for me to prepare for him."

"Of course he isn't. So we'll have to distract him."

"What do you have in mind?"

"Something big and splashy. How confident are you that your enemy—who is it, by the way?"

"I'd rather not say."

"That's not an option. I need to know what we're dealing with here."

"I'm not giving up his name. I could be wrong," he said, turning away so she wouldn't see the lie in his eyes.

"I doubt you're wrong. I can't really help you unless I know all the facts," she said. She got up from the computer. They'd had clients before who didn't do a full disclosure. To be fair, the way their agency was set up they usually worked with clients who were hiding something. Or who had done something illegal, and couldn't go to a government agency.

"Until I know for sure, I'll keep it to myself."

"I feel silly calling him your enemy."

"It's not too late to change your mind and stay here in D.C. In fact, now that I've seen your home I think it would be wise for you to stay here."

"Yes, it is too late. I'm not hiding out while you go set yourself up."

"Why not?"

"For one thing, I gave my word. And Liberty Investigations never quits until the job is complete."

"Your word is your bond?" he asked.

There was a tone in his voice that she couldn't place. "Yes, it is."

"I like that about you."

She arched one eyebrow at him, knowing she should just let this drop but unable to resist a little flirting. A little chance to see if she could get the upper hand with him the way he had with her when he'd kissed her in his car.

"What else do you like?"

"About you?"

"Yes."

"That you're tougher than you look."

It was exactly the right thing to say. She didn't know if he'd stumbled onto that secret of hers or if he was being genuine, and she didn't care. For once she was going to just go with the flow. She wasn't going to analyze it.

"But not tough enough to know the name of your black-mailer?"

"Let it go."

"I can't. I'm stubborn when it comes to things like that."

He walked around the command center, pacing like a caged animal. She realized she was pushing him and she didn't have any idea how he'd react.

"I can't stand this . . . waiting."

She glanced at her watch and then went back to the computer. She text-messaged Justine to get an estimate of when the plane would be ready. Justine's response was two hours.

"Did you mean what you said earlier about sparring with me?"

"I always mean what I say."

She rolled her eyes. "Come with me."

"Where are we going?"

"To my workout room. I think it'll be a nice distraction from all the waiting."

"I can think of a few other things that would distract me."

"Yes, but I'm not into casual sexual encounters."

"I promise it won't feel casual."

She could believe that, which was precisely why she was

leading him up the stairs and down the hall to her workout room.

She opened the door and nodded toward the changing room on the left. "There should be a Gi in there that will fit you."

"I can fight in these clothes."

"We're not fighting, we're sparring. There's a difference."

"Not to our enemies."

"Do you want to spar as we are?"

"No."

He crossed the mat to her. "I don't want to spar at all. Get your things so we can get to the airport."

"Daniel, I've heard that the gut should be our inner compass. And right now every instinct I have is telling me we need to give the team time to go over that plane."

"I don't want to hide. And my enemy will definitely know that I'm hiding."

"We're not hiding, we're regrouping."

"Then why the sparring?"

"To distract you. I can feel the anger pulsing through you."

"You can?"

"You seem outwardly calm but there's a tension in your shoulders and a real fire in your eyes. If you don't want to spar with me, you can beat the hell out of that punching bag. But I think you need to do something before we get on the plane for five hours."

He stood still in the center of the room, watching her, and she wondered if she'd said too much, if she shouldn't have kept her opinions to herself. But she'd never been one to stay silent.

"You might have a point."

"I'll let you in on a little secret," she said to distract him.

"Yes?"

"I'm always right."

"Funny thing, so am I."

"Well, we can't both be this time," she said.

"Exactly, so pack your things and let's get out of here."

"Why are you so stubborn about this?"

"Because he's taking down my house, Charity. Every time I evade him or his assassins he goes after someone else close to me. I'm not going to let go of my anger because it's what I need to make sure I don't lose focus."

"I can't see you losing focus—everyone needs to breathe to keep their center, their balance."

"Not everyone. I need a fight, a real fight with my enemy. And no matter how tempted I am to spar with you, I don't think this is the right time."

"Give me his name and we'll leave."

"You're not in charge," he said. "And we've already been over this."

She was smart enough to know when to back down. And she knew Anna was working on Daniel's past. She'd find this person who was threatening him and then maybe Charity would find the answer to why he was reluctant to name his enemy. And maybe even the real truth as to why he didn't want to gather his strength before confronting his enemy again.

Chapter Six

Self-deception remains the most difficult deception.
—Joan Didion

Charity didn't kid herself that she wasn't deep in self-deception mode as she left Daniel in the workout room. She had seldom met any man that she couldn't get around. But she was reluctant to use the attraction between them as a tool.

Which really ticked her off. She palmed her BlackBerry and dialed Sam's number.

"What's up, Charity?"

"Justine needs time to vet the plane before we get to the airport but Mr. Williams won't stay put. He wants to be out there like a moving target."

"So?"

"Sam, I'm his bodyguard. My main objective is to keep him alive. I can't do that if he insists on countermanding everything I tell him to do."

"I can send Justine in to cover him," Sam said. "Move you to a more strategic role."

"I don't want that."

"What do you want?"

"I want him to let me do my job."

"Charity . . ."

"Don't say it, Sam. I'm not treating him like anything other than a client."

"That says otherwise."

She pushed open her bedroom door and stalked to the closet. "He's trying to protect everyone else. He seems to have no regard for his personal safety."

"Has he given you any reasons for that?"

"Just says that he's dealing with an old enemy . . . who he won't name. Can you get the name?"

"I'll try. Anything else?"

"No."

She hung up with Sam and quickly packed her bag. She had a weapons bag that she always kept ready and it was already in the Rolls downstairs. She glanced around the room that her mother had decorated for her when she'd been twenty. It had been completed three short weeks before her parents' deaths. The room, with all its classical feminine touches, was like getting a hug from her mom every time she came in here.

She dialed Justine's cell next. "We're coming in about thirty minutes."

"We're not clear yet. I found something strange loaded onboard," Justine said, clearly distracted by the work she was doing.

"What?"

"I'm not sure yet. I think it's a tracking device but it could also be a listening mechanism."

"When will you know for certain?" Charity asked, reordering what they'd need to do. She needed more information from Daniel and if Sam came up empty she was going to have to . . . treat him like she did other men. Her mother was the first one to teach her that a pretty girl could open doors, or, in this case, gather information, with just a smile.

"By the time you get here. Why aren't you staying put?"

"He won't."

"Does he want to die?"

Maybe he did. With Daniel it was hard to tell what was going on inside his head. She only knew that as long as there was a breath in her body, she wasn't going to let him get himself killed. She suspected that was why he'd hired them. To make sure he had backup for whatever crazy, angry strategy he'd come up with. Too bad he played his cards so close to the chest . . . because she needed to know what was going on in his head.

"No, it's not like that. Just be ready for us."

"I will. You okay?" Justine asked.

"Fine."

"You don't sound fine."

"I am." This was her job, and she needed to find a way to push Daniel out of her mind and make him a client. With a job, not a man who fascinated her, she'd do better. Even Perry had never affected her this way. "This has just been a weird day."

"You can say that again," Justine said under her breath.

"What happened?" Charity asked, suspecting it was something personal because nothing rattled Justine on the job.

"That cop asked me out."

"Are you going?"

"Hell, no. I don't date law-enforcement types."

"You're not the kid you once were," Charity said.

"Whatever. Give me a call when you're at the airport. I want to make sure I'm ready before you come in."

"I will. Where's Anna?"

"She's here, doing something to the computer flight plan program."

"What?"

"Filing a dummy flight plan so you won't have to worry about anyone shadowing you in the air."

"Should I call her?"

"Nah, everything's under control here."

She hung up with her friend and glanced around the room one more time. She had every item she'd need for this job. Maybe too much stuff, considering she'd packed for a week and Daniel was determined to get this over with as soon as possible.

She rubbed the back of her neck, aware of the tension building in her. The tension that had been there all day long and was now getting worse.

Why should it matter to her if her client wanted to end the threats on his life in any manner possible, even by dying?

Daniel returned to the command center as soon as Charity left. Anger was like a hot lance inside of him and had been for the last three days since he'd realized that Sekijima was still alive and after him.

He knew his old friend well enough to know that he wasn't just toying with him. He was tearing down the house that Daniel had built from the ashes of Sekijima's old empire. Causing him to lose face. Daniel wasn't Japanese but he'd been so much a part of the Yakuza that he knew in his soul he was.

Daniel went to the weapons cabinet and opened it up. She had an arsenal . . . that shouldn't turn him on the way it did.

He fingered the samurai sword that hung there. It looked like one made by the Matuza. He had one in his own collection in the San Juans. Swords weren't used in fighting much anymore but he'd always liked the way they felt in his hands. He suspected that was because he'd first learned to kill with a knife.

Maybe he should have taken this break she offered, this respite, but he didn't want a break.

He had to keep moving so he could focus on his anger and not remember that he'd betrayed Sekijima first.

He didn't regret his actions . . . wouldn't let himself. There were some lines that should never be crossed, but at the same time, he did regret the loss of the man he'd once considered a brother.

"Do you like the sword?" Charity said, entering the room soundlessly. He glanced over his shoulder at her and realized she'd put something on her lips that made them glisten. He bit back a groan. His eyes fixated on her mouth . . . on her luscious mouth. Hell, if she'd suggested spending an hour in her bed instead of the workout room, he suspected he wouldn't have turned her down.

"Yes. Are you trained with it?"

"With all these weapons. I started training when I was twenty."

"In college?" he asked.

She shook her head. "No, I . . . I was a model so I traveled around doing jobs and partying."

"How did you go from that life to this?" he asked, needing the distraction of talking about her. But the truth was, he was fascinated by her. By everything about her. And he knew that he should leave her. Get further away than he'd agreed to.

Protecting her by keeping her with him had seemed like a good idea at the time, but now he wondered if there wasn't more to it. Had he kept her around because of lust?

"Um . . . something happened," she said. She walked over to the computer and sat down.

Dismissing him. But he wasn't the kind of man to be set aside. "What happened?"

"My parents were killed." Her fingers moved over the keys, opening her e-mail program and sorting through the messages there.

"Car accident?" he asked.

"No. Murdered for their money and jewelry by some street punk when they were in Japan," she said, opening a photo from the e-mail program. "I didn't have a chance to ask you if you recognize this woman."

He leaned in close over her shoulder and stared at the woman who'd shot Alonzo. He didn't know her but there was something familiar about her and her features. She reminded him of one of the wakushu—gang deputies trained as assassins.

There was something cold in her almond-shaped dark eyes that he recognized, harkening back to his own time working for Sekijima. Dammit, he felt that old life drawing on him. A part of him wanted back in that world. At least there he could act.

Life was so much easier when you went after what you

wanted and took it, instead of spending hours in meetings and negotiations. But another part of him, the man who covered his tattooed back in thousand-dollar shirts and suits, knew that he'd made a choice a long time ago and this life . . . was the one he had to continue to lead.

"I don't know her."

"We can't find her in any of our domestic databases, but Anna will run her through the international ones. Daniel, can I ask you something personal?"

"Sure."

"I guess I meant, will you answer?" she said.

"Depends on the question."

"How did you lose this finger?"

"Accident," he said. He and Sekijima had entered Dragon Lords as candidates together and worked their way up the ladder. One mistake early on had cost him that finger but he didn't regret the loss. It had made him the man he was today. A man unwilling to back down and focused.

"Accident? What kind?"

"The kind where you lose a finger."

"Daniel . . . why are you shutting me down? You came to us for help."

Charity watched him retreat, his green eyes going completely blank as he moved away from her. She sent the picture of the assassin to her BlackBerry so she'd have it with her.

Every question she asked him, he evaded neatly, keeping her not only at arm's length but in the dark. And that was a very dangerous place to be with a hit man on the loose. There had to be a connection between Daniel and the blackmailer that was more than just an illegal business transaction.

"For your own safety, there are some things that you aren't prepared to deal with."

"Probably," she said, "but I don't think we're going to be dealing with an infectious disease or a baby."

"What are you talking about?"

"Those are the two things I'm not prepared for," she said.

She almost teased a grin out of him and it felt good. She needed to find a way to make him trust her. And she wanted that trust to come from a bond of . . . well, friendship, if nothing else.

"I've been thinking more about what happened behind the hotel. I think Alonzo was the target."

Daniel said nothing.

"Is it gang-related?" she asked at last, pivoting to face him.

"Why would you think that?"

She closed the distance between the two of them, walking straight up to him. He didn't back down, which didn't surprise her. "Just ruling out possibilities."

"How is that a possibility?" he asked.

"Everything's a possibility until we cross it off."

"What kind of gangs?" he asked.

"You tell me."

He shrugged. "I'm a CEO—what do I know about gangs?"

"Your fingertip is missing."

He arched one eyebrow at her.

He'd reacted too strongly to her suggestion that there might be gang involvement, and there was only one reason she could assign to that. She ran through a list of gangs that she knew from the West Coast, quickly eliminating any that didn't deal in trafficking from other countries. Mexicans would bring their goods up over the border or perhaps in through Canada. Japanese would need a ship. It was hard as hell to get stuff from Asia into the U.S. without one.

Japanese meant . . . Yakuza. She knew precious little about the Japanese gangs, other than that they were thought to be modern-day descendants of the samurai. And she knew that they prided themselves on their loyalty to their gang and their boss . . . someone called the Oyabun. Gang members had elaborate body tattoos that weren't visible when they were dressed. And sometimes had severed fingertips.

The fingertips were given to a higher-up in reconciliation for mistakes. Now, Daniel wasn't Japanese, but . . .

"Are we dealing with the Yakuza?"

For a moment his eyes flashed with her answer. A terse nod of his head was all he gave before turning away from her.

He wasn't going to give up any information easily, she knew that. But this one piece . . . the Yakuza . . . dammit, that was going to be hard. They were a closed society. Hard to get information on because they didn't let their people leave alive.

He was afraid of showing any weakness—most men were, but she added in the fact that his enemy was going after those closest to him, striking at the housekeeper and now his security chief. The Yakuza was the only thing that had made a certain kind of sense.

"Do you have a criminal past?"

"No," he said.

She knew he was lying and cursed herself for asking the question so baldly. She sent a quick e-mail to Anna, telling her to focus on the Yakuza. And then shut down her computer.

"Are you ready to go?" she asked. If she stayed with him another moment, she was going to be tempted to force him to answer her questions. She shook her head. What was she going to do, beat the truth out of him? That was a line she wouldn't cross. Justine, however, would. She gave a brief thought to asking her friend to do just that, but she had a feeling that Sam would not approve. And she also suspected that Daniel wasn't the type of man not to hit back, no matter that the person beating him was a woman.

"Not yet. Don't dig into this, Charity. The past has no place in what's happening now. Your job is to protect me. That's it."

She let go of her own anger. Smile, she thought. Use the femininity that men never fail to respond to.

"You're not even sure you want me to do my job. And you won't listen to me," she said carefully. She turned to face him, looking up at him from her chair. "I just want to help you, Daniel."

"I'm your boss," he said. "Just do what I tell you and we'll be fine."

But she knew there was more to it than that. Daniel was the kind of man who was very used to getting his own way and he wasn't about to let a woman tell him what to do.

"You're a smart man," she said. "And I wouldn't dream of telling you what to do in the boardroom, but here . . . in this situation, I have more experience than you do."

"That's not it," he said.

"Then what is?"

"Control's a big thing for you," he said.

"I'd say I'm in good company then, because you refuse to back down. Don't forget it, buddy. I'll do whatever I have to in order to keep you safe. Even if that means digging all the way back to samurai days and the inception of the Yakuza."

He gripped her arm hard, drew her body close to his, glaring down at her. "There are some things that aren't meant to be brought forward."

What was he so afraid of in his own past? "The past always shapes who we are now. We can't run from it or it will consume us."

"That's a very Zen thought."

"Yes, it is. But it's also true."

"In certain circumstances, but I refuse to be defined by what happened years ago."

"We've all made mistakes, Daniel . . . don't worry about what we'll find."

He let her go, stepping away from her. She followed him, knowing that she was close to getting some answers. Needing those answers now more than ever.

"Tell me. Whatever it is, I need to know if I'm going to keep you alive."

"It's nothing. There's no big secret. Dig around in my past

all you want. But stay away from the Yakuza. The Oyabun doesn't take kindly to anyone sniffing at their door."

The Oyabun was serious business. For the first time, she felt a frisson of fear for Daniel. She had utter confidence that she could protect him but if his enemy was that powerful, nothing short of death would stop the man. And his death would simply bring about another enemy. Another person to take up the blood vengeance.

"You're going to have to trust me sooner or later."

"No, I'm not. Because we're going to take care of the threat to me and then you'll be out of my life."

"If you are an enemy of an Oyabun, this isn't going to go away easily."

"Let me worry about that."

She shook her head, grabbing her back and walking out of the command center. She heard him behind her as they walked out the front door. She paused to reset the alarm on the house.

"I really don't like you right now."

"Good. Don't like me. Don't try to figure out what's going on here. Just do your job and keep me alive so I can take care of business."

She gave him a steely-eyed look as he brushed past her, but he totally missed it because he concentrated on getting into the car.

"What's your plan when we get to the airport?" she asked. "Parade around until someone else takes a shot at you?"

"If I thought that would work, I'd try it," he said with a grim smile. "That way we could finish this now."

"You want it finished?"

He arched one eyebrow at her.

"Then give me the name of your enemy."

He held the door open for her and she tossed her bag into the backseat of the car.

"Tell me, Daniel. It's the only way to get him. Quickly and efficiently."

Chapter Seven

True guilt is guilt at the obligation one owes to one-self to be oneself. False guilt is guilt felt at not being what other people feel one ought to be or assume that one is.

—Ronald David Laing

Laing was definitely onto something with his thoughts on guilt, and Charity couldn't help but believe that was at the heart of what drove Daniel. His silence about the name of his enemy made her believe strongly that there was more to the threat.

"His name is Sekijima. But you won't find him in any of your government databases. Trust me on this."

"Why is he coming after you?"

"Revenge," Daniel said. "Get in the car. Even though you have the security fence, I don't like being out in the open."

She slid in the backseat and Daniel followed quickly behind her. She didn't know Henry and couldn't trust the man, so she knew they'd have to wait to continue this discussion when they weren't in his presence. The scent of Daniel's aftershave was strong and lingered in the air.

"Take us to the executive airport, Henry," Daniel said as soon as he was seated.

"Yes, sir."

"Tell me more about your parents' death," he said, as they left the compound and entered the residential area. Henry drove with skill through the traffic. His change of topic told her that he didn't trust the driver, either. But that didn't surprise her—Daniel really didn't trust anyone.

Charity kept one eye on the cars around them. "Why do you want to know?"

"You said our past shapes who we are," he said gently.

That's right, she had. "I was very shallow back then."

"You were young. Twenty is just not old enough for maturity."

"Well, I never felt that way. I mean, I'd been traveling and socializing for over five years in the super-model crowd. I was an only child and my parents were very indulgent."

"You were their princess?" he asked.

She felt a twinge of shame at how spoiled she'd been and how she had taken that for granted. She'd wanted for nothing growing up. Materially her parents provided more than one child could ever play with. And emotionally, they'd doted on her and she'd returned that love. Until she'd reached her teenaged years.

"Definitely. My father had insisted that I get an education and I had attended a boarding school in Switzerland before I started modeling. He wanted me to continue but I talked him out of it."

When word had reached her of his death, she'd been haunted by guilt and her own arrogance. She'd expected to have a lifetime to find her way back to her parents, to live up to their expectations, but everything had changed in a moment.

She'd left Paris, where she'd been working and living, and traveled to Kobe, where her parents had been killed. The local police didn't have any leads on who was responsible for her parents' deaths, and she'd stayed there, working for almost two years training under an aikido master and asking questions. Becoming so much a part of the town and the people there that eventually she'd found the answers she'd sought.

And once she'd had a name, she'd honed her skills until she was able to go after the man who'd killed her parents—and bring her own retribution to him.

It was after his death that Sam had found her. He'd completed her training and offered her a chance to work for justice, not as a vigilante. She'd accepted and never looked back.

"Did you ever go back to school?"

"I have a degree in business administration. But working for Liberty Investigations, I don't really use it. But, yeah, I have it, and I'd like to think that maybe he knows I do."

She felt so exposed sitting next to him, thinking about her parents. She knew it was the vulnerability that remembering them always brought to the fore.

"What about you? Are you close to your parents?" she asked. The file they'd had on him didn't mention any family at all. Her family had defined how she'd lived her life and where she was now. She didn't like to dwell on them, because that was the past. She tried hard to always keep looking forward and moving forward.

He rubbed his thumb over the tip of his distorted right forefinger. "My parents . . . I never knew them. My earliest memories are of living on the street."

"Oh, Daniel," she said. The picture she had of him suddenly reshaped and changed. She wanted to touch his distorted finger, to take it in her hand and rub it the way he did.

In his eyes she'd seen that there was more to the man than the GQ clothing and urbane sophistication, but she'd never have guessed at this type of past. Factoring the Yakuza connection . . . she didn't like where this was going. If Daniel had once been a part of the a gang, then he would never be able to get out.

"What? It wasn't bad. I learned at an early age how to survive and I've never forgotten those lessons."

"I imagine you haven't. No wonder you are so successful." She felt every inch the spoiled, pampered girl she'd been. True, she'd changed once she'd reached adulthood, but there were times when she was embarrassed by the girl she'd been.

"How do you mean?"

Why had she started this conversation? She didn't need to

know the details of his past in order to guard him. Yet she couldn't help herself. She was curious about what made Daniel Williams who he was.

"You learned early to go after what you wanted and not let anything stand in your way."

He glanced over at her and she felt something pass between them. It wasn't sexual but it had a tinge of that in it. It was more a soul-deep recognition.

"I guess so," he said.

"It took me a while to get there. I expected my life always to be perfect," she said, tucking a strand of hair behind her ear. "I feel so silly saying that to you."

Daniel turned to her and she felt her breath catch as he watched her. He looked at her like she was so much more than the sum of her parts. Like even though he now knew her shameful past, he still saw her as someone of integrity.

"You don't strike me as someone who feels silly often." She liked the way his voice sounded when he talked quietly. Keeping the conversation between the two of them made it feel so much more intimate than it probably was.

"True. But in light of the kind of life you must have led—"

"Don't belittle your upbringing. We all have scars we carry with us. Even if they don't show on the surface, it doesn't mean that they aren't painful."

She bit her lower lip and leaned in close to him. "I liked you better when you were making passes at me."

"Liar."

"Maybe." She fought the urge to smile at him. She wanted to believe that she was keeping one step ahead of him but he read her like an open book.

"No maybe about it," he said. "You don't respect anyone who can't see past your curves."

Charity wanted to ask him if her respect was important, but she was very afraid that he'd say yes. And even more afraid that she'd believe him.

* * *

Henry accelerated and weaved through the cars on the highway with more than skill, driving with more speed than he had been before.

"Is there a problem, Henry?'

"Someone's following us, sir."

Daniel was glad for the distraction. Charity was too much of a temptation. He wanted to make promises to her that he knew he'd never be able to deliver. But she made him long for a life and for a path that he'd never experienced. Never wanted before he'd stared into her gunmetal-gray eyes.

"Slow down and let them catch us."

"Yes, sir."

Charity gripped his arm. "Are you crazy? We don't know who's in the car."

"We will when they catch us."

"Daniel—"

"I'm in charge, remember?"

"You're looking for a fight," she said, under her breath. But he noticed she reached for her weapon. As had he.

"Where is the car, Henry?"

"Black Spider. He's keeping his distance but he's been back there since we left Ms. Keone's residence."

Charity turned around. With the tinted, bulletproof windows, there was no way for the driver of the other car to notice her attention on him.

"Can you make out a plate on the car?" Charity asked.

"No."

"What's your plan, Daniel?" she asked.

"Henry, pull off the road up here. We'll sit and wait."

"As your bodyguard—"

"They'll probably drive past. How good a shot are you?"

"I'm a marksman."

"I think a flat tire would help us," he said.

She nodded. "What will you be doing?"

"Hoping the driver presents a target."

"We need him alive to question."

Daniel didn't say anything. Henry eased the car to the side of the road and Charity opened her window to set up her shot. She was on the right side so the car would be going by on the left. She knew that she'd have to time her shot just right.

She didn't pay any attention to Daniel or to Henry. She had her job to do and she would get it done. She saw the cars flying past at over 70 miles per hour and waited for the black Spider.

As soon as she saw the taillights she took a breath, let half of it out, and squeezed the trigger. The silencer muffled the sound and she felt it kick in her hand. A second later the car lurched as the right rear tire started losing air. The driver didn't slow down but kept moving.

She memorized the license plate and then glanced over at Daniel. Henry was already pulling back out into traffic. "Are we trailing them, sir?"

"Yes."

"Did you see the driver?"

Daniel had memorized the face. He had little hope of actually recognizing anyone Sekijima sent after him. All of the people who'd been close to the Oyabun years ago were taken down when Sekijima was.

He wanted to know how long Sekijima had been working on rebuilding. Then he'd have a better idea of how loyal and well-trained they were. Loyalty, though, he knew would not be easily shaken. The blood bond that brought the Yakuza together was one that few were ever able to betray.

"I didn't recognize him."

Henry pulled out, following after the car.

"I'll watch our back," Charity said. She kept her weapon palmed and ready, though she didn't relish the thought of any type of high-speed shoot-out on the busy interstate.

Henry accelerated and she was thrown off balance as he

quickly changed lanes. Daniel steadied her. "Put your seat belt on."

"I can't see what's going on behind us if I do that."

"Then I'll watch. I don't want you injured."

"I'm fine. You're the priority here."

"You're not fine while Henry is trying to catch the Spider. Put your seat belt on."

She braced herself on the seat with one foot on the floor. "Now, I'm fine."

And she was. As Henry weaved between two more cars, Daniel took her arm and physically turned her in the seat, reaching across her body and drawing on her belt. It snapped into place with a solid click. Then he adjusted the strap, his fingers lingering over her right breast.

She brushed his hands away. "Why is this important to you?"

"Car accidents kill."

"So will anyone who's trailing us. I need to be free to do my job."

"You will be. Henry, give up the chase and take us to the airport. We'll see if anyone else follows us there."

She shook her head at his stubbornness. "This isn't going to work."

"What isn't?"

"You protecting me," she said, taking a stab in the dark. She was beginning to suspect that the only reason he'd changed his mind was so he could keep her safe from his enemy.

"It's working fine so far."

Charity crossed her arms over her chest, but she still held her weapon in one hand. Instead of looking pouty, she looked like she was getting ready to shoot someone.

"I'm the boss," he reminded her.

"You take a little too much pleasure in that."

"It's the only way I can win with you."

She uncrossed her arms and tilted her head to the side, studying him. "Is that important?"

He arched one eyebrow at her.

"You can be such a man sometimes."

"That's because I am one. Henry, do you notice anyone behind us?"

"No, sir. But I was doing some evasive maneuvering early to try to catch the Spider. I'll slow down now."

"I don't want you to drive directly to Mr. Williams's jet's hangar when we get to the airport."

"Yes, ma'am."

"What are you thinking?" Daniel asked.

"That my team needs time to get into place and see who follows us if Henry's skillful driving didn't warn them off."

Daniel stroked his thumb over the nub of his forefinger. He had absolutely no idea what Sekijima would do next. He hated that his old friend had the advantage on him—Sekijima knew him better than anyone. Knew everything about him from the time he was a young boy.

"What are you thinking?" Charity asked, her voice soft and low, startling him out of the past.

He shook his head. "Nothing important."

"Daniel?"

"Hmm?"

"I'm never going to lie to you, even when it might be easier than telling the truth."

"Good. I'm glad to hear that."

"I expect the same from you," she said. "If we're both going to stay alive we have to have trust between us."

He had no response for her. He'd trust as much as he was able to—which wasn't a lot. He just didn't trust. Even with Sekijima he hadn't. But then, the Yakuza had bred him to trust only himself. In business he'd survived and prospered because he always played his cards close to the vest.

"Can you do that?" she asked.

"No."

"Is it me? Do you think I'm not trustworthy?"

Charity was the kind of woman every man dreamed of having by his side. The kind of woman who'd be a loyal and fierce partner. She was good-looking and had the kind of manners that money just couldn't buy. He knew—he'd tried to.

She was so much better than he was on so many levels, and he hated that his inability to trust had been interpreted to mean something else by her.

"It's not you I don't trust. I thought I already told you that."

"You did. But a lot has happened since then. I think we need to communicate better so we're not missing any clues."

"If I think you need to know something, I'll tell you."

"Like you did with Sekijima's name," she said, almost whispering. He knew the sound of her voice didn't carry beyond the two of them.

"Yes."

"What were you just thinking about?" she asked. "And don't say *nothing*—you looked too fierce."

"Maybe I was thinking that you needed a strong hand," he said, capturing her wrist and rubbing his thumb over the inside of it.

"Strong hand?"

"I didn't stutter."

"You'd better be prepared for a heck of a fight if you try to discipline me."

"Under the right circumstances, I bet you'd be amiable."

She shook her head. "Why does everything with you come back to sex?"

"Why do *you* always think it does?" he countered.

But he'd moved closer on the seat. He wanted her. And he wanted her safe. Already he was planning a way to make sure she was out of harm's way when he challenged Sekijima. He'd probably have to do something that she'd find unforgivable to cause her to drop her guard.

He studied her fine features, memorizing them for a time in the future when memories of Charity would be all that he had left. He didn't understand why he felt so strongly about her. Didn't think he ever would, but then women were meant to be mysterious.

"It frightens me when you stare at me."

"Why?"

"Because I can tell you're not at all the sophisticated, civilized man you pretend to be."

He almost laughed at that. She was too observant, but then he hadn't expected that to change. From the first moment she'd walked into his hotel room, she'd been knocking him off balance.

"Good, forewarned is forearmed."

"Do I need to be armed around you?" she asked, in that silky tone of hers that made the hair on the back of his neck stand up.

"Aren't you always armed around men? Ready to charm or disarm them?"

"Maybe."

"I thought we were going to have honesty between us."

She put her free hand over his wrist, right below his watch, and stroked his arm. "Yes, I am exactly like that. But with you it's different."

"How?"

"I got the feeling you saw past all that."

He drew her hand up toward his lips, brushed his mouth over the back of her hand. The skin was soft; her nails were painted a delicate color, yet that hand had held a Sig Sauer semiautomatic with surety and skill. God, she intrigued him.

Chapter Eight

Everybody's at war with different things . . . I'm at
war with my own heart sometimes.
                                              —Tupac Shakur

Tupac's rap had a way of cutting straight to the heart of what she was thinking. Charity didn't find any peace in knowing what was in her own heart. She wanted to pretend that she didn't understand Daniel or that she wanted just his body or to protect him.

But the truth was that she felt sometimes that there was nothing left inside of her except the two parts that warred with each other. Nothing left of that girl who'd been her family's pampered princess. That all of the real Charity had been burned away in her quest for vengeance against the man who'd ruined her world.

The man who'd dared to take her perfect fairy tale and ruin it. And she hadn't been subtle about ruining that man's life. She'd been very Old Testament about her quest against Kenkichi. She'd gone after his parents, and then after him. She'd taken his world apart as efficiently as he had hers.

The only problem was that she'd emerged not knowing who she was anymore. And she still didn't know.

She doubted that knowledge was going to come to her now as she stared into Daniel's green eyes.

"What are you hiding?" he asked her as he dropped her wrist. He brought his hand up to her face, something he did with too much frequency. She was starting to really like the way he held her jaw in his hand. That ruined forefinger moving over her skin softly, tracing the line of her jaw.

"Nothing," she said, the honesty of that statement rattling around inside of her.

"Charity," he said, her name released on a breath.

"I'm not lying."

"I know. You're not empty."

His words scared her. How could he know the very fear that had always driven her?

"How?"

"It's in your eyes. You think that you are—"

She jerked her head away from him. "Don't tell me what I think, Daniel. You don't know me."

"Sweetheart, you don't even know yourself," he said.

His words were at once sweet and cutting. She shook her head, angry that she'd let him distract her from her focus. It didn't matter that she'd wanted to distract him. She had just realized that with Daniel she was playing a game she didn't know how to win.

But she was beginning to understand the rules. "You needle me when you want a distraction."

"I'm not needling you."

"That's right, you aren't."

He gave her one of those half-smiles of his. "When we get on the plane I want you to help me think like my enemy."

She sat up straighter. Finally, something she was good at. Once she understood more about Sekijima she could figure out what made him tick. Her own knowledge of the Yakuza was rough, barely formed. Kenkichi hadn't been in the Yakuza and he'd been the only thing she'd focused on in Japan.

Her training had taken her into sex clubs, and she'd met a few of the local gang members but she hadn't allowed her focus to slip. She needed to bring that focus to bear now. She needed to find a way to tap into that same single-minded determination that had brought her to her quest against Kenkichi ten years ago.

But she didn't like that part of herself. Hadn't wanted to admit that behind her pretty face and body there could lurk a need for such revenge. Yet there had been.

"I'll help in any way I can. What I don't know, Justine will."

"What are the strengths of your team?" he asked.

"That we're all so different. We all think and fight in unique ways. Justine is a street fighter—"

"Like me," he said.

"Yes, and she has no give in her. She'll fight using whatever means are necessary. She's a dirty fighter when she has to be."

"And the other girl?"

"Anna lives by the rules, but she's smart enough to outwit anyone. I've never seen anything like it. She hates to fight and she almost never has to."

"And you?"

"I'm lethal with weapons. I don't like getting personal in a fight the way Justine does."

"You keep yourself above it," he said.

Was that true? She thought about the way she relied on her weapons, the fact that she could make a kill or take someone down without getting in too close. And when she had to, she used martial arts training to quickly subdue her opponent.

"I guess I do."

"Why is that?"

She shrugged. "I've never analyzed it."

"Would you like to hear what I think?"

"No."

"I never would have figured you for a coward," he said.

"I'm not going to let you goad me into this. I'm not scared of anything you have to say."

He turned to the front of the vehicle and the silence built

between the two of them. And just as she was sure he'd planned, she couldn't stop wondering why he thought she fought the way she did.

He wouldn't be right because there were things about her that no one knew. Not even Sam, with his extensive connections, had ever been able to find out what made her tick.

The glimpses of vulnerability he caught so fleetingly crossing her face made him want to stand up for her. Tell her not to worry about whatever faults she imagined she had, because he knew she was so much better than he was.

"You are so used to wielding your looks and lethal talents that most people don't know how to deal with you—and you like that."

"Are you sure? It could be that people really just don't know how to deal with *me*. Most women are afraid to trust their husbands and boyfriends around me."

"Is their fear of you or the men?" he asked, leaning closer.

She shrugged. "What does it matter?"

"I want to know."

"I think it's a mixture of both. Usually they are right and their men make a pass when we're left alone. So it's not that I'm hiding, exactly—it's just that . . ."

He loved the cadence of her words and the softness of her voice. In all his life, softness had been absent. Even now, with all his wealth and supposed security, he still hadn't found any way to bring that into his life.

"Every time you let someone in, they disappoint you," he offered. He wished they'd met two months earlier. Hell, two *days* earlier would have been great. Any time before Sekijima had resurfaced, and he could have courted her the way she deserved. Instead he was going to have to use her as cover to set up a trap that could endanger her.

Well, didn't *that* make him the catch of the year!

"I'm not complaining. Most of the time I come on full-out bad-ass to scare people. It's easier that way."

He wanted to laugh. She was so blasé about her life, which was borderline extraordinary. Her cell phone beeped and she pulled it out, read an e-mail, and then quickly typed a response on the keypad.

"Justine is ready for us at the plane. I alerted her that we might have a tail. She's getting into position to protect our back until you are safely on the plane."

"That's fine. Henry's not going to be able to drive out in this car."

"I'll have Anna take care of him."

Henry stopped the car and got out to open the door. Daniel signaled him to wait. "Your people will have to keep him safe for a few days."

"We will," she said.

"I've rethought keeping you with me, Charity."

"Not again."

"It'll be safer for you if you stay here with Henry."

"You're not paying me to stay safe. You're paying me to protect you."

"Since I'm the one paying, I get to choose," he said, capturing her wrist when she would have started to get out of the car.

"If I answered to you," she said. "But Sam is my boss and he assigned me as your bodyguard."

Henry opened the door and she swiveled on the seat, turning her legs to exit. "You're a very caring man—to watch out for your staff the way you do."

She climbed out before he could answer. Caring wasn't something that was in his makeup, but if she wanted to believe that about him, he wasn't going to argue. He knew enough about women to know that they were more comfortable with emotion.

He wanted Henry safe for two reasons: one, the man had

been a good driver over the last few years; and two, he wasn't sure that Henry wouldn't talk if he were captured. He'd probably give them Charity's address, and he wanted that information kept out of Sekijima's hands.

"Henry, someone from the Liberty Investigations team will take you to a safe location until the men who were after me are caught," Daniel said.

"I'm fine, sir. I know how to watch my back."

"All the same, I'm going to insist you take a few days off—think of it as a vacation."

"Yes, sir."

He followed Charity across the tarmac, thinking about what she said. He'd revealed more to her than he'd intended, and though she thought that would help in her investigation, he knew that it had increased the danger to her.

As soon as the plane was in the air, Daniel took out his laptop and started working. He'd taken a call as soon as they'd arrived at the airport. Charity wasn't sure if she was glad that he was unavailable or not.

She did know she had a list of questions that just kept growing, questions that only he knew the answer to, questions that her gut warned her were going to stay unanswered.

"Why didn't you take him to your dojo and work out some of your frustrations on him?" Justine said as she settled into the leather executive chair next to Charity.

Charity exhaled, trying to find the right words. "He wasn't agreeable to that."

Justine chuckled. "That man is getting under your skin."

"I don't know why," she admitted. "Did you have a chance to run the Yakuza and the name he supplied us with?"

"There's nothing on Sekijima in our databases, but Anna only had time for a prelim search before we took off. She's back on the computer working her magic again. We'll have an answer soon enough."

"Good. I e-mailed you the plans for his house on that island in the San Juans as well as the high-rise apartment. Can you make a list of everything we'll need to secure those two locations?"

"Will do. I think security is going to be tough at both locations. You're good but that island is vast. Will he wear a vest?"

"I doubt it. It would be better if we could get a decoy in to take his place. I'm going to add that to my security-plan scenarios."

Both women worked on their laptops independently until Justine needed more information from Anna and left to go chat with her.

Daniel didn't move from his desk, which took up one wall of the plane. Charity stretched and scanned the interior. She knew that Anna and Justine had been over every inch of the plane but she wasn't going to be satisfied until she had a chance to check out the small bedroom in the back and reassure herself that there was no danger lurking there.

She'd been up front to check out both of the pilots and felt she could handle anything those two threw at her. The one flight attendant in the back with them had worked with Liberty Investigations before.

Charity saved the document she'd been working on and stowed her laptop. She went over to Justine and Anna.

"What's up?" Anna asked.

"I want to check out that room. Can you cover Daniel until I'm back?"

"Sure. But we already went over it."

Charity shrugged. "I've got to see for myself."

"Go ahead—we've got him covered."

"Thanks."

She entered the room and realized there was a lot of space for an assailant to hide. The bed was king-sized and took up all of the room from wall to wall. There was a small closet, which was empty of everything save Daniel's suit jacket. The small washroom was also empty, but as she went over the space she found a small pin.

Bending down, she picked it up. It was similar in size to a Rotary pin, but the design wasn't familiar.

"What are you doing in here?"

She glanced up from where she was kneeling on the floor. "Double-checking."

"For?"

"Anything that can help me keep you safe." He leaned there in the doorway against the frame, his arms crossed at his chest, staring down at her.

She stood up and turned in the close confines to face him. The pin felt cool in her hand and she turned it over in her palm, glancing back down at it for a minute before lifting her palm toward him.

"Do you recognize this?" she asked.

His face went totally blank as he stared down at the item. Then he picked it up and brought it closer for examination. "Where did you find that pin?"

"On the floor," she said, indicating a spot behind her. His eyes had gone totally quiet when he stared at the pin. There was a history there and she had no idea what it was.

He closed his fist around the small symbol and pocketed the piece. He kept his hand in his pocket and she wondered what he was thinking. Wished like hell there was some way to know what was going through his head. Did it have much significance?

"Wait. That's evidence. I want to dust it for prints," she said. Would he say something more?

"It's not evidence."

"It isn't?"

"No, it's a warning."

"Then you know who dropped it here?"

"I know who left it."

"Sekijima?" she asked. She wanted to know more about the

man who was threatening Daniel. Anna was going to run a check on him but if he was deep in the Yakuza, they'd only get so far.

"More likely one of his people."

Charity leaned her hip against the countertop surrounding the sink. "Why would they be that clumsy?"

He shook his head, drew his hand out of his pocket, and looked down at the tiny pin one more time. His mind was somewhere else. Probably on the enemy he knew far better than he wanted to reveal to her. "They weren't. This was left in here deliberately as a signal to me."

She didn't like the way his fist was clenched. The anger was back, that cold and fierce tension in his shoulders and eyes. He looked dangerous and she knew it wasn't directed at her but all the same she was concerned.

She thought about what he'd said . . . a signal. This felt more and more like a game of cat and mouse to her. A deadly game to be sure, but a game nonetheless. What was Sekijima up to?

"You say it's a warning of some kind?"

"Yes, it is."

She waited, hoping he'd elaborate, but Daniel wasn't much of a talker and revealed only what he wanted to.

"Will you let me give it to Anna? She can punch the image into the computer and trace it."

"She won't find anything," he said. "This is an inner circle pin. The kind that only those close to the Ōyabun have."

"Then how do you recognize it?" she asked.

"Because this pin was mine."

Chapter Nine

*The most fundamental way a woman can misunder-
stand a man—and the misunderstanding with the most
far-reaching consequences—is to think that she can understand him at all . . .*

—Mark Leyner

The words of Mark Leyner danced through her mind as she
stared at Daniel. "You mean you had one like it?"

"No, this was my pin. See this chip in the paint on the
side?"

"Yes."

"I can remember the scuffle I was in when that happened."

"How deep where you in the Yakuza?"

"Deep enough not to answer any of your questions."

"Daniel. This isn't just about trusting me . . . this is about
your safety."

She stopped leaning against the sink and stepped forward
to implore him to tell her everything. And the plane hit an air
pocket, driving them both off balance.

Daniel reached for her, steadying her with a hand on her
arm. But they hit a second one, throwing her body into his.

He fell backwards, landing on the bed. His hands came to
her waist, holding her against him. She put her hands on his
shoulders, lifting her upper body so she could see him.

"Finally I have you in my bed," he said, holding her firmly
and rolling until he was above her. His hips settled between
her thighs; his arms braced on either side of her body kept his
weight from crushing her.

She could have countered his move. Could have rolled him back under her, but she didn't want to. In this moment, close as they were, she saw something in Daniel's gaze that she hadn't really glimpsed before. A touch of real emotion.

"I thought you were going to tell me more about the pin."

"Do you really want to talk?" he asked.

He traced his finger over her cheekbone and then down over her lips. "I can't believe that someone so beautiful can be so lethal and yet at the same time so real."

She closed her eyes because he was too close and his words touched her deeply. Maybe he didn't mean them to have any weight beyond a means to seduce her. "It's just a physical arrangement of features . . . something my parents passed on to me through their DNA."

His touch moved from her lips to her eyebrows, tracing each one. Then she felt the warmth of his breath and his lips against her skin. His mouth moved in the same path his fingers had down the side of her face.

Her lips tingled as he neared her mouth. Her eyes opened and she watched him as his tongue brushed over her lips, tracing the seam between them. She parted hers, inviting him to come closer.

He lowered his head and she arched her back so she could respond better to his kiss. Tipped her head to the side so their mouths fit perfectly. A tingle of excitement shot down her spine and she reached up, gripping his shoulders as his mouth moved over hers.

This kiss was different from the ones they'd shared earlier. They had been about him proving to her that he didn't need a woman as a bodyguard or about her proving that she could handle him. But this was a sharing.

A sharing of something she couldn't define and didn't want to.

She wanted to just close her eyes and let herself be swept

away by the passion that Daniel felt for her. And it *was* for her. Daniel saw the real woman behind all the smoke and mirrors.

She pushed her hands into his thick hair, holding him to her while he plundered her mouth with his lips and tongue.

His hands swept down the sides of her body, skimming over the curves of her breasts and lingering at her nipped-in waist. One of his hands slid between their bodies and she felt again that minute touch of his fingers sliding over her skin, tracing the deep vee of her blouse.

His fingers skimmed over the rounded globes of her breasts, slipping beneath the fabric so she felt the heat of his touch on her bare skin.

She bit her lower lip as he found his way under the fabric of her bra. But he stopped then, letting his fingers rest against her left breast. Anticipation had her arching her back, offering herself to him. But he held still, waiting for something she couldn't define.

She looked up at him and their gazes met. Her breath left her in a rush and something passed between them.

"Take off your shirt," she said. She'd been longing to see his chest since that first little aikido encounter in his hotel suite. There was strength in Daniel—real strength. She'd been going out with senators and businessmen for too long.

No one like Daniel. She wanted to experience everything she could in the short time they had together. And she didn't kid herself about that. They were essentially too different for this to last.

She started to pull back, to draw away from him, but then he shifted his weight to his left arm and reached between them, the backs of his fingers brushing her breasts as he unbuttoned his shirt. She shook from the brief contact and bit her lip to keep from asking for more.

His chest was hairless and free from tattoos or piercings but it wasn't smooth. There were scars. One long, jagged one ran over his left pec. She traced the rough skin where it looked like someone had tried to cut out his heart.

She lifted her eyes to his, questions burning on the tip of her tongue, but he quieted them with his finger on her lips. "Not now."

She lifted her head and found the tip of that scar with her tongue. She pushed against his shoulders and rolled to his side, lying next to him on the bed. She traced the scar with her finger and then feathered light kisses over it. It was thick and she knew from experience that it would have been deep and painful.

"Knife wound, right?"

"Yes, how did you know?" he asked, his fingers on her face while she caressed his chest.

"Tough cookie, remember? And I have one like this," she said.

"Show me."

She tugged her blouse from the waistband of her skirt and lifted the hem so he could see. She'd gotten the wound her first night in Kobe, but she didn't want to dwell on that. As soon as she lifted her blouse, Daniel rolled her under him again.

He skimmed his fingers over her scar and then lowered his head to taste it. He used the edge of his teeth as well as his tongue, and for the first time ever she found her scar to be sexy and desirable.

She didn't dwell on the fact that she was starting to believe that Daniel might just be the kind of man who accepted her— really accepted every part of her.

Daniel concentrated on seducing Charity and tried to ignore the pain he felt at the thought of her being knifed. He knew she could handle it. She'd proved throughout the day that she was tough as they came, but a part of him . . . okay, all of him, wanted to find the bastard who had hurt her and rip him apart.

What the hell was that? He wanted her in his bed because she was gorgeous and he wasn't in the habit of denying himself anything he wanted. Why did he care about her? Hell, *did* he care about her?

He looked down into those crystalline gray eyes of hers and knew he did. He tried to force himself back into the moment, but even sex couldn't detract from this. He didn't care about anyone. Not really, but suddenly here she was, and he did.

Not now, he thought.

"Daniel?"

"Hmm?" he said, lowering his head to kiss the base of her neck. He hated talking, especially now. The scent of her skin was like a potent aphrodisiac and he breathed her in.

He imagined he was inhaling her strength and beauty. Imagined that he was taking her into his skin and making her his own. And that was the only place she could really stay with him—in his imagination. He was meant to walk a solitary path in this life.

He unbuttoned her blouse, running his finger down the center of her body. Over her sternum and between her ribs. Lingering on her belly button and then stopping at the waistband of her skirt.

He slowly traced the same path upward again. This time his fingers feathered under the demi-cups of her ice-blue bra. Barely touching her nipples, but they both beaded. A shaft of desire pierced him, shaking him to his core.

Blood pooled in his groin, making him hard. He laid his hand over her breast and felt the beating of her heart, swift and strong. She scraped her fingernails lightly down his chest. As he moaned, the sound rumbled up from his chest.

Sex always made him feel powerful. Watching a woman react to the body he'd honed and kept in optimum shape was a powerful rush. But Charity was his match. She was soft where a woman should be, but her muscles were also defined. There was real strength in her body.

And he wanted to lose himself in it.

She nudged him onto his back and he fell to his side and let her explore.

His muscles jumped under her touch. He tried to hold still and not reveal anything, but doubted he succeeded. All she'd have to do is glance down at the erection straining against his pants.

She circled his nipple with her fingernail, tracing the line where it met the smooth skin of his chest. Then she scraped her nail down the center line of his body, following the fine dusting of hair that narrowed and disappeared into the waistband of his pants.

"No need to ask if you like my touch," she said, a little breathlessly.

"I do," he said, sitting up and drawing her into his arms. She straddled his lap and when her center met his cock, he groaned deep in his throat.

He reached around her back and unhooked her bra and then pushed the cups up out of his way. He pulled her closer until the tips of her breasts brushed his chest.

"Charity." He said her name like a prayer, holding her against him.

She shifted on his lap, but he held her still. His hard-on nudged at her center. He shifted her around until he could get his hands under that short skirt that had been driving him crazy since the first moment they'd met.

Her legs were smooth and soft, and as he skimmed his hands upward, he encountered a sheath holding a knife wrapped around her left thigh. It shouldn't have been a turn-on but it was.

He kissed his way down her neck and bit lightly at her

nape. She shuddered, clutching at his shoulders, grinding her body harder against him.

"God, baby, I want you," he said against her skin.

"Me, too."

He stopped caressing the flesh around her knife and slid his hands higher. Encountering the cool skin of her buttocks, he traced the crease between them down to her honeyed center. The gusset of her panties was damp with her desire. He traced the opening of her body, her wetness branding his skin.

Her mouth opened over his and he told himself to take it slow, to make this last, because he knew that he wasn't going to have another chance to be alone with her. When they landed in Seattle he was going to have to push her away so Sekijima couldn't use her against him.

But all he wanted was to pull her closer, and right now he could. And did.

He slipped one finger into her channel and felt her clench against him. Her hips shifted, so he slid deeper into her.

She captured his face, tipped his head back, and kissed him, her tongue thrusting into his mouth as he added a second finger to the first inside her body. She rocked against him and he pushed himself deeper into her humid core.

He used his thumb to find the pleasure of her center and stroked her as she rocked against him. He was so hot and hard he thought he was going to burst when she caught his lower lip between her teeth, biting carefully as she rocked harder against him.

He used his free hand to cup her butt and urge her to a faster rhythm, guiding her motions against him. He bent his head and his tongue stroked her nipple, and then suckled her.

Everything in her body clenched. She clutched at his shoulders, rubbing harder and tightening around his fingers as her climax washed over her. She collapsed against his chest as he held her close.

*   *   *

Daniel had never seen anything more beautiful than the woman in his arms. She was so responsive to his touch and he wanted more.

She tried to push his shirt off his shoulders, but he rolled her under him so she couldn't. His arms and back were covered with traditional Yakuza tattoos. Two large dragons battled for supremacy on his back and arms. His chest had never been tattooed. He'd been planning to get one, but had gotten out of the gang to start his new life before he had any ink done there.

"I want to feel your naked skin against mine," she said.

"Stay on top and you will."

"I don't take orders," she said.

Her breasts were full and her skin flushed from her recent orgasm. He ran his hands slowly over her torso, almost afraid to believe she was really in his arms.

Her nipples were tight little buds beckoning his mouth. He'd barely explored her before and he needed to now. He needed to find out how she reacted to his every touch. He caught both her wrists in his hands and brought them behind her back, holding them in one of his hands so that her breasts were bare in front of him and there was nothing she could do about it.

"That's perfect."

"Daniel, let me get my arms free," she said.

"Not yet."

He pulled her to him and lifted her slightly so her nipples brushed his chest. Holding her carefully, he rotated his shoulders and rubbed against her. Blood roared in his ear. He was so hard, so full right now that he needed to be inside of her body.

"Daniel, please. I want to touch you."

He realized then that there was something very fragile inside this ultracompetent and professional woman. He pulled her more fully into his arms, cradling her to his chest with one arm. She closed her eyes and buried her face in his neck. Each exhalation went through him. God, he wanted her.

He was so hard and hot for her that he was afraid he might come in his pants. But he was going to wait. Then he felt the minute touches of her tongue against his neck.

He also felt the bite of her nails against his own wrist. Charity wasn't going to just let him dominate her, and he liked that. She was his equal here in bed. He brought both hands to her back, lacing their fingers together to keep her where he wanted her. But when she rotated her hips against his, he knew he wanted more.

He wanted her naked in his lap. He let go of her hands and reached under her skirt and drew her panties down her legs. She shifted to one side and then the other until he had them free of her body, her breasts swaying with the movement.

She still wore her shoes and her knife sheath. Her skirt was bunched at her waist. She slid her hand down his chest, unfastened the button at his waistband, then lowered his zipper.

Hot damn!

Her hand slid inside his pants and encountered his naked skin. He'd never been able to tolerate too much clothing. Her touch was smooth up and down his length. Tightening his hands on her back, he glanced down at his body and saw her small hand burrowed into his pants, saw her working him with such tender care that he had to grit his teeth to keep from ending it all right then. But he wanted to be inside her the next time one of them climaxed.

Glancing down, he saw her smiling up at him. Little minx. She was getting back a little of her own and he didn't mind at all.

His breath caught in his throat. She was exactly as he dreamed she'd be: nipped-in waist, long, slender legs, and full breasts. He nudged her over on her back.

She smiled up at him. He leaned down, capturing her mouth

with his as he shoved his pants further down his legs. She opened her legs and he settled between her thighs.

The humid warmth of her center scorched his already aroused flesh—he thrust against her without thought. Damn, she felt good.

He wanted to enter her totally naked. At least this first time, but that was a huge risk and one he knew better than to take. His life was a danger zone and creating a child was a risk he'd never take. He was intimately familiar with how harsh the world was to unwanted kids.

He pushed away from her for a minute, then fumbled with his pants, taking them all the way off. He found the condom he'd put in his pocket earlier today.

He glanced over at her and saw she was watching him. The fire in her eyes made his entire body tight with anticipation. He put the condom on one-handed and turned back to her.

She opened her arms and legs, inviting him into her body. He lowered himself over her and rubbed against her, shifting until he'd caressed every part of her.

She reached between his legs and fondled his sac, cupping him in her hands as he shuddered. He felt weakened by her power over him. He wanted this woman, and in ways beyond the physical, which was something he'd never experienced before.

He needed to be inside her now. He shifted and lifted her thighs, wrapping her legs around his waist. Her hands fluttered between them and their eyes met.

He held her hips steady and entered her slowly, thrusting deeply until he was fully seated. Her eyes widened with each inch he gave her. She clutched at his hips as he started thrusting, holding him to her, eyes half closed, head tipped back.

He leaned down and caught one of her nipples in his teeth, scraping very gently. She started to tighten around him, her hips moving faster, demanding more. But he kept the pace slow, steady, wanting her to come again before he did.

He suckled her nipple and rotated his hips to catch her pleasure point with each thrust. She fit him like a velvet glove, clenching down hard on him each time he retreated. Her hands were in his hair, clenching as she threw her head back, his name escaping her lips. He closed his eyes, gritted his teeth, and did everything in his power to hold back his own climax until he felt hers ripple through her.

Thrusting faster, he leaned back on his haunches and tipped her hips up to give him deeper access. Her body was still clenching around his when he felt that tightening at the base of his spine seconds before his body erupted into hers. He pounded into her two, three more times, then collapsed against her. Careful to keep his weight from crushing her, he rolled to his side, taking her with him.

He kept his head at her breast and smoothed his hands down her back, knowing his gut had been right—this woman was the one who he wanted to bleed for. And he was very afraid that Sekijima was going to give him his chance to do just that.

Chapter Ten

Each one's pleasure draws him on.

—Virgil

Charity didn't know that Virgil was a hundred percent right, but lying pressed to Daniel's side she felt like she had found a place where she could rest forever. She knew it was an illusion, that safety and home weren't things that lasted. But for this one moment she wanted to close her eyes and enjoy it.

But her mind wouldn't let her. It was already racing back to what she'd discovered before they'd made love. That pin. He'd used his body and her lust to distract her.

The sweat had barely dried on her body. He was still partially clothed and she was naked except for her bunched-up skirt and her knife.

He was tracing a path down the side of her body, lingering on the curve of her breast and again at the knife. Many men found the tough sides of her personality hard to swallow, but with Daniel she really sensed that was what drew him to her.

She leaned on her elbow, seeing her blond hair fall over her shoulder, and touched his. His hair was dark, his skin tanned . . . so different from her paleness. They were a study in contrasts. Yet she knew they were more similar than either of them wanted to admit.

She traced the scar on his chest. She had a million questions about it and was coming to know him well enough to know he wouldn't answer them.

"I still have some questions," she said softly. With any other man she would have already figured out how to deal with him. Either to be the bubble-headed blonde or the tough-as-nails badass. But with Daniel she didn't want to play a role.

"I know."

He rolled away from her and sat up, buttoning his shirt. She reached for her bra and drew it on, glancing up when she felt his hand on her side where her scar was.

"How'd you get this?" he asked, his rough fingertip tracing it.

"Knife fight. Same as you."

"I meant the circumstances," he said. Standing up, he disposed of the condom in a trash receptacle built into the wall near the head of the bed.

He drew his pants up over his legs, tucking his shirt in.

"Why don't you wear underwear?" she asked.

He almost grinned—she saw his lips twitch as he fastened his pants. "I don't like it. Any other questions along that line?"

"Nah," she said, standing up and letting her skirt fall down. She found her panties and drew them up her legs.

"I do like yours," he said. She felt his hand on her backside as she maneuvered her thong up over her thighs and over the sheath.

"Thanks. I do have more questions."

"Finish getting dressed and I'll do my best to answer them."

"Promise?"

"Tell me about the knife fight and yes, I'll answer your questions about the pin."

He was so specific, but she wanted the answers about the pin so she nodded her head. She didn't like to talk about her past. She was willing to bet that Sam and her aikido master were the only two people alive who knew about those days in Kobe.

She drew her blouse on over breasts and skin still sensitive from his touch. She fastened it quickly, then walked over to the bathroom mirror to check out the damage. Her lips were swollen from his kisses, but there was little she could do about that.

She tucked her blouse in and met her own gaze in the mirror, needing to see something on her face, an indication that she hadn't made a big mistake by sleeping with this man. This client. Oh, God, she'd never done this before, never even been tempted. Despite her relationship with Perry, she'd never before been intimate with a man she was guarding.

"Charity?"

"Yes?"

"Are you okay?"

She glanced over her shoulder at him, saw him standing there next to the bed with the rumpled comforter. If not for the messed-up bedsheets, there would be no indication that anything untoward had happened. He was put back together and looked as if . . . nothing of importance had taken place.

Was she just another woman he'd slept with? No, she thought. She was his bodyguard, and it was about time that she started acting like it.

"Fine. You were going to tell me about the pin," she said, forcing her mind back to the case.

"Knife fight first, remember?"

"How could I forget? I think I mentioned that my parents were killed by a street thug."

"Yes, you did. Were you with them when they were held up?"

"No, I wasn't. But I flew to Kobe as soon as I learned of their deaths. They had been my world . . . Anyway, I arranged for the bodies to be brought back home, and after the funeral I returned to Kobe. The local police weren't conducting much of an investigation, so I started asking questions."

"What a dangerous thing to do," he said, almost under his breath.

"At the time I didn't realize it. I stepped on someone's toes and this," she said, rubbing her side, "was a warning for me to back off."

"Did you?"

"No."

Daniel had never known the area around Kobe well. His gang had been U.S.-based with extensions in Japan, but he'd also stayed in the States where he was best used. In Japan he stood out, but he wished now he'd gone there. Wished now he had the connections to find the person who'd "warned" Charity so he could give them a little warning from him.

"What did you find out?" he asked at last, realizing he was staring at her. She looked a little leery of him now. Which was probably exactly what he deserved, but he didn't like seeing fear in her eyes when she looked at him.

"The name of the man who'd mugged my parents."

"Who was it?"

"It doesn't matter anymore."

"I want to know."

"It's part of my past, Daniel. Are you ready to talk about yours? We could make another bargain. Otherwise, I want to hear about the pin."

He wasn't going to give up information about his past, but he was going to find out more about hers. He made a mental note to contact Alvin Myers, the head of his I.T. department and a man who could find more secrets than the government if the money was right.

"What do you want to know about the pin?" he asked, shoving his hand into his pocket. He fingered the pin. There was so much of his past that he'd shoved away so he could move on. Move away from the Dragon Lords and Sekijima. But it was always with him, right up until the last few days, when he'd realized Sekijima was still alive and coming after him.

He'd thought he'd moved on, that he'd left the street thug behind and become the man he pretended to be.

"Can I see it again?"

He handed it to her. She lifted it up, studying the colors and symbols. "Let's go back into the main cabin where I can jot down some notes."

"Your lipstick is gone," he said, suddenly not wanting anyone else to know what had transpired in this room. Holding Charity in his arms was something highly private to him. He doubted he'd get the opportunity to do it again but it was already something he cherished. He'd had so few things to actually call his own. He wanted this to stay between the two of them. And only between the two of them.

"I know."

So be it, then, he thought. He should have known better than to try to be a gentleman. He wasn't one, and clearly Charity didn't expect him to be.

He pushed past her to open the door but she stopped him with her hand on his arm.

"I haven't done anything I regret."

"Me, either. I just don't want the world to know."

"Why? Are you embarrassed by me?"

He shook his head. As if he could be embarrassed by the finest woman he'd ever seen. Not only physically fine and beautiful, but also good deep inside. And that was the one thing he'd never had. Never even cared to have until he met her.

"Never. But I want this to be private. Something only the two of us share."

She wrapped her hand around his upper arm and rubbed her cheek against his shoulder. "It is."

"Good," he said, cupping the side of her face and holding her there for a long minute. "Once we go out there . . . be on your guard. The flight attendant and pilots don't work for me. Sekijima has contacts in every level of society. He'll know we were together."

"I'll be with you, Daniel," she said, her voice a gentle reminder.

"In case we get separated," he said, warning her, wanting her to be on her guard. He realized he had to say more and couldn't once they left this room. "Sekijima isn't like anyone you've ever faced before, Charity. Now that we've been to- gether, he'll know and he'll use that to destroy me."

"Don't, Daniel. Don't worry about me. I really am tougher than I look and I've survived situations that others haven't. I'm going to keep you safe from Sekijima and his threats."

"Don't worry about protecting me—take care of yourself."

"Uh, I was hired to protect you," she said, lifting her head. "You talk about him like he's some kind of demigod . . . he's just a man and I've never met one who doesn't have a weak- ness."

She was good at analyzing people and situations. If anyone could find the flaws in Sekijima, he thought, she might have a chance. The man whom Daniel had known was different from the man who was coming after him today.

"He's been a loyal member of the Dragon Lords for as long as I've known him. He's brought in new members, strong members who have strengthened the power of the gang."

Charity nodded. "He holds a position of power and it sounds like he earned his way up to the top."

"He did. Through blood and sweat and other things you shouldn't know about."

She shook her head. "I probably already know more than I should. Where is he based? In Seattle like you are?"

"No. Vancouver. But that doesn't stop him from reaching back to Seattle."

"Were you in his gang . . . the Dragon Lords?"

"He's not with them anymore," Daniel said. He'd kept that secret hidden for too long to give it up now.

"Who is he with?"

"I have no idea. That's why I was reluctant to name him. But this pin leaves no doubt that he's the one behind the blackmail and the death threats."

"Why don't you know where he is now? Did you lose contact with him?"

He turned to face Charity, then looked at this room that for a few brief moments had felt like a sanctuary in the craziness of his life. "I don't know, because he's supposed to be dead."

Charity understood that Daniel was talking to her now because he was afraid of being overheard in the other room. Secrecy was very important. She knew that and respected it. And she needed his story so she could figure out how to handle the threat from Sekijima.

Though she was functioning as his bodyguard, she was also a top-notch analyst. She knew how to get into the minds of her enemy and usually could figure out what their next move would be. With Sekijima, her hands were tied to some extent because she'd never dealt with the Yakuza before.

But Daniel had. And he understood them far better than she suspected he wanted to admit.

"Are we dealing with the real man or does someone want you to think we are?" she asked. Questions were key to understanding. Most of their clients didn't like questions because they had their own secret fears that they had done something to bring on the threat.

"I have no idea. All of the moves that he's made feel like Sekijima to me. The list of people who knew him and know me is very small," he admitted. He wouldn't look at her but kept his gaze slightly over her shoulder.

"How small?" she asked. What wasn't he saying? Was there something he was avoiding telling her? Some reason that she couldn't see or understand? Despite the fact that she'd shared her body with Daniel, he was still essentially a stranger.

"Nonexistent. The two men who did know us both are dead."

"Are you sure?"

"I saw them both lowered into the ground with my own two eyes."

Which meant that Sekijima was still the main suspect. Daniel was too sure of who he was dealing with. Every move he took was isolating more and more people from him. She was guessing it was his way of protecting those around him.

"Who's at your homes?"

"Staff-wise?"

"Yes."

"No one. I gave them all a paid leave until this blows over."

"We're going to make this happen quickly, Daniel. Once Liberty Investigations gets involved, we don't waste time. You'll have your staff back and your life back in no time."

"Is that a promise?"

"Yes, and I always keep mine. Do you want to tell me about the pin in here? I'd rather let Justine and Anna hear about it, too, because I think they could add some insight. But the flight attendant doesn't work for us."

"I've used her before but I have no idea of her loyalty."

"We can send her in with the pilot and co-pilot," Charity suggested. "Or bring them both in here."

"No. I don't want to do anything else behind closed doors until we are on the ground and on my turf."

Where he could control the variables, she realized. "Sounds good. So, the pin?"

"If she's working for Sekijima, she already knows about it. If not, the information will get her killed."

"Then let's do it in here. I can catch my team up on it later."

"You know the longer we stay in here, the more they are going to think we're still on that bed."

"So?"

"I wish we were."

Daniel made her want to curl up next to him and just stay there. There was something in his eyes that said he was entranced by her, and she knew she was entranced by him. She was starting to need him. Liked being in his company so much that she had felt a little twinge of happiness when he'd said that he wanted them to stay in the room by themselves to discuss the background of the case.

She shouldn't let it mean so much. She knew she was setting herself up for a fall, tried to caution herself that there was nothing real between her and Daniel. But when he caught her hand and drew her down onto the bed next to him, she knew that there was.

No matter what the past had taught her, this man was becoming important to her. It didn't matter that she'd only known him a few hours—he was having a real impact.

He opened her hand where the pin was and used his good forefinger, the perfect one, to point to the different designs on the face of the pin.

"This symbol is the one for the Dragon Lords," he said, pointing to a very Japanese-looking dragon. "These colors signify power, fidelity, and face."

"Face is like pride, right?"

"Sort of. I don't think anyone who's not Japanese can ever really understand what it means."

"Do you?"

"Yes."

"Daniel, you're not Japanese."

She said it delicately and teasingly. If she had to guess, given his coloring and physical attributes, she'd say he was of Italian or Latin heritage.

"In all the ways that count, I am."

"Were you fostered to a Japanese-American family as a child?" she asked. He'd said he grew up on the streets but this was the United States. No child was left alone like that.

"Not really fostered. But I did rescue a boy from being beaten by a rival gang when I was about eight."

"How did you rescue him?"

"I was big for my age and I'd been fighting since . . . well, since I could remember. The kid was small and I almost walked away."

Charity understood immediately that he was sharing something important from his past. It was the way he spoke. His words quick, the inflection flat.

"Why would you walk away?" she asked.

"Prolonging death is like torturing someone. And if I helped that kid live one day only for him to die the next . . . what's the point?"

His life was like nothing she'd ever imagined. She knew that life was tough for some people. She'd always felt blessed and lucky to have been brought up the way she was. But until this moment she hadn't realized just how lucky she'd been.

"So you rescued him. Then what happened?"

"Um . . . two really big bad-asses entered the alleyway where we were."

"Were you afraid?" she asked.

"Probably, but another part of me was just relieved. I'd been waiting every day for that kind of fight."

"What kind?"

"One I wouldn't walk away from. I'd lived longer than I expected, and to be honest, in those days life was hard."

"You must treasure the comforts of your home and your success," she said.

"Hell, no. They are trappings that could easily be ripped away from me."

"Oh, so what happened next?"

"The punks were the older brothers of the boy I'd helped out. They took me home with them and gave me food and a place to sleep."

He didn't say it, but she suspected they'd also given him a family. A way to belong after he'd been alone for so long.

Chapter Eleven

*Being in motion, not knowing what's going to hap-
pen next, not only suits me but has become an unlikely
vehicle for faith.*

—Holly Morris

Charity was always on the move. Always looking forward so she didn't have to stop and maybe look back at what she'd become and how she'd changed. Staring into Daniel's eyes made her realize that she wasn't alone in that—the two of them had been honed by their pasts. But she didn't think her life had been anything like his. There was something too raw about Daniel when he spoke of his childhood.

And even the horror of losing her parents the way she had wasn't the same as what he had endured. She ached for him and wished in some way that she could make up for what that little boy who had been Daniel had lived through.

She wrapped her arm around him because as he'd been talking, he'd stiffened and drawn more into himself and she wanted to hold him. She wanted to let him know that she was here now. And though she knew he'd rebuff her if she promised to make the future . . . wait a minute. Was she really thinking of the future with him?

Could she be?

No.

Well . . .

"Charity?"

"Hmm . . . ?"

"Why are you holding onto me?" he asked. He didn't pull back from her.

She dropped her arm. "I want to comfort the little boy that you were."

"He wouldn't have accepted it."

"You mean *you* wouldn't have," she said carefully.

There was something guarded in his eyes and she was surprised he let her glimpse it. He was the most self-contained person she'd ever met. Lord knew, there were times when she wished she had that ability to shut her emotions off. She wondered if he'd teach her how, but would have felt silly asking, so she kept quiet.

He shrugged, then ran his finger down the side of her. She already liked that touch too much. No one touched her the way he did—it made her feel special.

"You don't have a peachy background, either. Your transition into womanhood was rough," he said.

She could tell that it mattered to him. "We have that in common, then."

"Don't, Charity."

"Don't what?" But she knew what he was going to say. She wasn't an idiot and the man was a loner. It wasn't just because of the threats he had received—it was something deeper, something ingrained in the very fiber of who he was. Given the way he grew up, it was amazing to her that he had made it off the streets and into the corporate world.

"How did you transition from street kid to CEO?" she asked.

"That's complicated and really has no bearing on what's going on here."

She drew back. "Fine. What else can you tell me about Sekijima?"

"Charity." There was exasperation in his voice and she hated that.

She wished they weren't in this cramped room with only a bed. A bed on which she'd just made love to him. And wanted to do so again. Damn, where had all her good sense gone? And what was it about this man that made her forget it?

"What?"

"I'm not the kind of person you want to find things in common with. I'm not a nice man."

She shook her head. "You are."

"Don't let what happened here—"

"I'm not stupid, Daniel. I know that you wanted me and I wanted you, too. I wasn't talking about sex."

He seemed shocked and actually pulled back from her. Of course, what had happened between them was on her mind. Her body still pulsed from his possession, and to be perfectly honest, she still wanted him.

"The way you take care of your staff shows me what kind of man you are. You've gone out of your way to ensure that everyone who works for you is out of harm's way while the blackmailer is still out there."

"Well, they aren't the intended victims. I don't like anyone to have to pay the price for my decisions or my mistakes."

"Me, either," she said. "And you need to stop treating me like you do your staff. I'm your bodyguard."

She pushed to her feet, pocketing the pin that she'd found. She would give it to Anna and let the other woman start investigating it. She'd turn up something—Charity was sure of it.

She opened the door, but Daniel reached around her and closed it with the flat of his hand. He pressed up against her, trapping her against the door, his chest resting heavily against her back. He bent his head down to her and spoke directly into her ear.

"Don't think you're only my bodyguard."

"I'm not?"

"I can't be the man you want to me to be, Charity. It's not that I don't want to, it's just that my life is a mess."

She grabbed his hand where it rested on her shoulder and bent back until she had enough wiggle room to turn. She knew he'd let her have that room and that irked her because she wasn't so sure she could best him in a hand-to-hand fight.

"You don't know what I really want. And I haven't asked you to be anything other than who you are. I . . . I don't sleep with clients normally, and this is the last thing I was prepared for with you."

He wrapped his arms around her, tucking her against his chest. "I know you don't sleep around. And I'm not trying to put words in your mouth."

"How many people have a pin like this?" Anna asked. Daniel was reluctant to talk about anything involving the gang, especially to other people. Old habits ingrained in the giving of his word, his blood, and the tip of his finger were hard to break.

He shrugged. "Exact numbers are never known."

"More than a hundred?" Justine asked.

He kept silent. Who knew? Gang numbers were private.

"It will help us to narrow down the search if we know what we are dealing with," Anna said.

"I've given Charity the name of the man I think is responsible. Start your search there."

"Daniel—"

"Ladies, you work for me. I hired you. Do what I'm asking you."

"We don't exactly work for you," Justine said.

Charity bit back a smile as she sank deeper into the leather seat and watched Daniel and her friends interact. He didn't give up anything. She knew he wouldn't. He'd give them exactly the information he thought they needed and not a shred more.

He was hiding something. And whatever it was, he'd deemed it unimportant to their investigation.

"Different facts may seem trivial to you, but when we

gather them together they might trigger something in one of us. We're not trying to be nuisances—this is how we operate. And why we're so successful at closing cases like this one," Charity said.

"I don't mind giving you information if I have it. But the exact gang numbers . . . that's not even available. I doubt anyone other than the Oyabun would have them."

"And you think that is Sekijima?" Anna asked.

Her fingers moved over the keyboard of her encrypted laptop. She scarcely looked up at either of them, but when she did, her eyes lingered on Daniel with a curiosity that had nothing to do with the case.

"Excuse me, sir."

"Yes?" Daniel said, glancing at the flight attendant.

"The pilot asked me to inform you we'll be landing in thirty minutes."

"Thank you," he said, dismissing the girl. She went back to the front of the plane.

Charity had kept an eye on the woman, since she was unknown to her and could be a variable in Sekijima's plan to take down Daniel.

"We can finish the conversation at my home."

"Which one?" Justine asked.

"The high-rise."

"Okay," Charity said. "Justine, did you secure the vehicle for Daniel to use on this end?"

"I have my own car," he said. "I don't like to be driven if I don't have to be. Charity, you can ride with me. Ladies, I'm afraid it's only a two-seater."

"Not a problem—we've got our own ride. I want to check your car before you leave," Justine said.

"Sam sent an operative to do that already."

Justine trusted no one. Sometimes Charity wondered if the woman even really trusted her and Anna. "He isn't someone I know. I want to go over it one more time."

Charity smiled to herself. Justine and Anna felt the same way she did about making sure Daniel stayed alive while they ferreted out his blackmailer and brought him to justice.

"I'm not going to sit somewhere and wait while you—"

"Yes, Daniel, you are. Car bombs are too easy to rig."

He started to say something but then stopped, gave her a tight nod, and then walked back to his seat in the middle of the plane. He took out his BlackBerry and started answering messages. She knew he was mad, but had no idea why.

With every new thing she learned about this man, it seemed she really knew less about him.

"What happened in the bedroom?" Anna asked softly, her British accent pronounced and proper the way it always was. Charity leaned her head back against the headrest on the chair and closed her eyes.

"We talked. I found that pin. And then I asked him some questions. He's hiding something."

"He's not the only one," Justine said. "What's going on between the two of you?"

"I have no idea," she said, being as honest as she could.

"He's a client, Charity," Anna reminded her gently.

"You think I don't know that?" Charity said. It was all she thought about—well, that and the fact that he still wouldn't come clean, not only about his past but about Sekijima.

"Don't jump on her. She's concerned about you. We need you one hundred percent on the job. Not acting like . . . well, not yourself."

"I am one hundred percent, Justine. This thing with Daniel . . . it's not something I'm deliberately doing. I can't explain what it is about that man. He's so damned frustrating, and yet, there's something about him."

Justine leaned down, resting her elbows on her legs, her thick black hair swinging forward around her face. "He's a man—of course he's frustrating."

Anna laughed. "My brother would argue that."

"Your brother's a dork," Justine said.

Angus wasn't a dork. He was a high-society playboy who was drop-dead gorgeous and lived his life like it was one big party. It was odd to imagine him and Anna coming from the same womb.

Justine and Angus always gave off sparks when they were together. There was something about him that needled her. Charity always enjoyed seeing her friend thrown off guard by the other man.

"That's neither here nor there. When we land, I'll secure the plane and keep Daniel here until you have had a chance to make sure his car hasn't been tampered with."

Anna typed a few last notes on her computer. "I'll go ahead to his residence and start going over the security. Want to meet there tonight and figure out the details of his plan to trap the blackmailer?"

"Sounds good."

Daniel was disgusted with himself as he sat safely on the plane with Charity while her friends made sure it was not dangerous for him to leave. Charity sat near the entrance to the plane. She wasn't relaxed but hypervigilant in what he was coming to recognize as her work mode.

She had her weapon held lightly in one hand and wore her small earpiece-microphone. Before they'd landed, all three women had changed into slim-fitting black leather pants and jackets.

Being a fighter, he knew they must have chosen the leather for its protective qualities. Being a man, he was instantly hard, looking at the black leather hugging Charity's curves. Though he'd promised himself the one time he'd had her on this plane would be it, he knew he wasn't going to keep that promise.

She'd drawn as little in life as he had. Money had been im-

portant for a long time because he'd grown up so poor. He'd
thought that being wealthy would be a solution to many of his
problems but he found that the problems were still there.

His cell phone rang and he glanced at the caller ID. Seeing
that it was Tobias, he was glad for the distraction that work
and their problems with U.S. Customs would provide.

"Williams."

"Tobias, here. There was a fire in warehouse number one.
The fire department has it under control. The warehouse
manager has smoke inhalation."

Fuck. "Is he going to be okay?"

"Yes. He's with the EMTs. They are going to take him to
the hospital for observation, but he'll be fine."

"How much damage is there?"

"They won't let me in until the fire department has had a
chance to finish looking over the site, but from the outside it
doesn't look too bad. It looks like those smoke alarms we in-
stalled last month saved our butts."

"Do they have any idea what caused the fire?"

"Not yet. I told them about the threats to you personally,
and they are going to be looking to make sure it's not arson."

He wished Tobias had kept his mouth shut, but given the
circumstances, he probably had made the correct decision.
"Have you called our insurance adjuster?"

"Not yet. Figured I should let you know what was going on
before you saw it on the news."

"The news?"

"CNN and the locals. There were huge black clouds of
smoke coming off the building. Since we store mainly empty
crates here or the fabric goods we import, they aren't sure
what caused the black clouds. But I overheard one of the fire-
men say that he suspected it was from some kind of chemical."

"A chemical that was used on the fabrics?" Daniel asked.

"I don't know yet. I'll call when I know more."

"Very good."

Daniel hung up the phone and saw Charity had come to stand over him.

"What's the matter?"

"Fire in one of our warehouses."

"Here in Seattle?"

"No, on the East Coast . . . New Jersey."

She nibbled on her lower lip and he could see her turning over this new incident in her mind. "Does he think you are still in D.C.?"

"I doubt it. He's showing me that he can strike at everything I own. That there's no place safe from his reach."

"It could be an accidental fire," she said. "It's improbable but we shouldn't rule it out."

Daniel knew it wasn't accidental. Sekijima was coming after him where he lived and worked. Doing his damnedest to tear apart the life that Daniel had built out of the wreckage of his last years with the Dragon Lords. He reached up and rubbed his shoulder, right where the tail of the ornate Japanese dragon tattoo was. That tattoo was the mark of a Dragon Lord and the mark of his one-time friendship with Sekijima.

"Yeah, I don't believe in coincidence."

"Me, either. Justine has finished checking the car and we're good to go."

He stood up and straightened his suit jacket to make sure he could reach his gun in his shoulder holster.

"Justine brought the Jaguar up to us. All you have to do is go out and get in. I'll drive, since I've had evasive and defensive driving training."

Daniel shook his head. His first job in the Yakuza had been as a driver—he knew better than anyone how to evade tails bullets. Plus, he knew the city like the back of his hand, and

Charity would be limited by whatever knowledge she'd gleaned from maps.

"Daniel—"

"There isn't a single thing you can say that will sway me. I'm driving."

"Why did you hire us if you were going to be like this?"

Why *had* he hired them? At the time he thought it would be great to have Liberty Investigations doing the legwork for him. But that was before he'd realized the extent of Sekijima's anger and how he was gunning for everything in Daniel's life.

Before he realized that he'd now made three more people vulnerable to attack from an Oyabun who'd always been the most ruthless man that Daniel knew. Ruthlessness was the one thing he'd understood from earliest memory. That and survival. Somehow, no matter what, he always survived.

There had been times when he'd expected he'd die, but somehow he never did. It gave him a feeling of invincibility and he still had it. He didn't know what Sekijima believed, but Daniel knew when he confronted his old Oyabun, he was going to make damn sure he was the only one who walked away.

"That's not relevant now. Will Justine or Anna be following us?"

"Um . . . no. Anna's already at the high-rise condo building and Justine's going to hang back here until the flight crew leaves."

He liked the way her team operated. They covered everything. "I'm beginning to think I hired you because you are the best in the business."

She gave him a cheeky, flirty grin, which made him want to kiss her and let his hands wander all over her body.

"Well, you'd be right about that. Are you sure you won't let me drive you?"

"Yes. It has nothing to do with my confidence in your abilities, Charity. I'm sure you're a top-notch driver."

"Really?"

"Yes, really."

"Then why can't I drive?"

He shook his head. He wasn't going there. Not now and probably not ever. He led the way off the plane and down to his Jaguar.

Chapter Twelve

Each man has an aptitude born with him. Do your work.

—Ralph Waldo Emerson

Charity's aptitude had always been a knack for reading people, even before she'd turned her grief into vengeance. The quotes running through her head gave her a semblance of balance. It was something that her mother had begun when she had first started going to school—giving her a little thought to ground her day. And it had never left her.

Right now she wasn't reading much from Daniel. One of the traits she really admired in him was his ability to be completely null, to keep his energy low and move through life almost unobserved.

His driving was exactly the same. He wove effortlessly through the traffic with an ease she wouldn't have had because she didn't know the streets of Seattle the way he obviously did.

"You're staring at me," he said.

"Am I? Maybe I'm just trying to pick up some tips."

"I doubt it. You already know everything about how to drive."

"Maybe I have some room for improvement."

Daniel took his eyes from the road for a second. "You're perfect."

Before she could respond, he was back to concentrating on

the job at hand. She wasn't even sure what he meant. Maybe she'd misunderstood him.

"I'm not perfect. I missed the hit man in D.C. I should have gotten her."

"We already covered this," he said. "Why do you keep returning to it?"

She didn't like to talk about the way she learned because she had to see her mistakes over and over in her head. She slowed them down and changed her actions in her mind. Tried different scenarios until she got a better understanding of herself and the problem she was struggling to solve.

"It's just what I do. I'll never make that mistake again."

"I don't doubt that. Why did you get into this business?"

She nibbled on her lower lip. "I have an aptitude for weapons and self-defense. It was a natural thing for me to do. After Mom and Dad were gone, I wasn't interested in modeling anymore."

"I'm not surprised by that. You have too much energy and smarts for modeling."

"It's harder than it looks," she said, defending her former profession.

"Is it?"

"Are you teasing me?" she asked.

"Maybe."

"Maybe? You run a multinational corporation—I expect a firmer answer than that."

"How do you know what to expect? Been around a lot of CEOs?"

"Yes, I have. We guard them a lot."

"In situations similar to mine?"

"No. You're different, Daniel," she said. Dammit, her voice softened and she hadn't meant for it to.

"I've always been different."

Given his background, she wasn't surprised he felt that way. It fit with who he was and it was one of the things that drew her. "Different isn't bad. I'm not exactly like anyone else, either."

"You can say that again. How did Sam find the three of you?"

Charity thought about her team. They all fit together so well that it made a certain kind of sense that they'd work together. They functioned so seamlessly she honestly couldn't imagine not working with Justine and Anna, though when they were first brought together she didn't think they'd last through their assignment.

"I'm not sure how he found us all, but he does have a knack for putting the right people together. We're like pieces of a puzzle that don't fit anywhere else. Anna used to be with MI-5 and Justine is a street fighter."

"And you?"

"Me? I was a . . . it's not pretty."

"I told you I grew up on the street. I can handle ugly."

She put her hand on his arm, squeezing gently because she had to touch him. She still wanted to comfort him and pull him into her arms, letting him rest there until the scars of his past healed and melted away.

He took one hand from the wheel and squeezed her hand on his arm. "Tell me."

"I was a vigilante. I used my anger to keep myself alive. I mean, I wanted to die after my parents were taken from me."

"Vigilante? Who'd you go after?"

"First was Kinkichi—he's the man who killed my parents. When he was no longer walking the earth, I thought I'd be able to breathe easier but that wasn't so."

"Vengeance is a hard thing to live with."

"Who did you take revenge on?"

Daniel didn't say anything, but she knew his silences didn't necessarily mean he wasn't going to tell her. After a few minutes he said, "Sekijima."

"Do you want to tell me why?"

"If I do, you'll be disgusted."

She shook her head. "No, I won't. Whatever is between the two of you is fueling what's happening now."

"It involves a woman."

"Most feuds between two men do."

Daniel glanced over at her, his green gaze hard. "Have you ever had two men fight over you?"

"Of course not. Men don't see me the way you do," she said.

"I highly doubt that."

She thought about it for a moment. "Well, I don't see them the same way I see you."

Charity had never let fear rule her life and she wasn't about to start now. She knew that she couldn't build anything permanent with Daniel, because his life and lifestyle were both in perpetual motion. He wasn't the kind of man who was going to ask her to give up her career and be a stay-at-home mom.

He seemed to have no designs on a little slice of domestic bliss. And to be fair, she didn't, either, but there was something about the man that just made her want to find a way to be with him forever. Forever? Who the hell was she kidding? She knew *forever* didn't really exist.

"So you were both fighting over a woman?"

"Not really," he said. "Yuki wasn't the type of woman to look at more than one man."

"You loved her?" Charity asked, surprised because Daniel wasn't the kind of man she would have guessed would let himself love anyone.

He shrugged. "What is love? I cared for her. We started living together when I went legit."

Went legit? She wanted to question him on that but knew better. Right now she needed to know about Sekijima, and for once he was willing to talk.

He shook his head. "Yuki was smart and funny. She was capable of holding her own with men. She didn't know about my past, that I came from the street."

"I'm sure that wouldn't have mattered to her," Charity said. She knew that his past made her admire him even more than his success in the business world. That kind of background made a man solid. She wouldn't have to worry about Daniel calling her a wannabe or expecting her to dress up and play a part in public.

"I'm not. Her family was wealthy and we were introduced by a very powerful man. Later I found out that she'd been ordered to continue seeing me."

His tone was completely flat and she couldn't tell if he felt no emotion or had just learned to hide it deep inside. She didn't exactly like hearing about this woman. No matter his tone or what he said—she was still jealous of Yuki.

And jealousy was a useless emotion. Besides, the woman clearly wasn't in his life anymore. But a part of her was jealous of the suppressed emotion in his voice. Whatever he'd felt for Yuki, a part of him still clung to it.

"She did what her family told her to?" Charity asked.

Daniel's lips twitched. She hoped he hadn't picked up on her envy, but she'd always had a hard time keeping her stronger emotions to herself. The only time she ever was able to completely disengage was during combat.

"Yes. But then she fell for me. It seemed like I was riding high. The business took off and was growing. I finally had money. A nice place to sleep each night. A woman to call my own . . ."

"What happened?" she asked, because from the beginning this story hadn't had a happily-ever-after feel. She tipped her head to the side and studied him, realizing that neither of them had found happily-ever-after. Granted, she wasn't exactly searching for it and she suspected he wasn't, either. But it had remained elusive for both of them.

"She . . . she wasn't what she appeared to be. She'd been sent to investigate the Yakuza by the U.S. government. Sekijima found out and warned me."

There was no good way for this to end—she knew Daniel wouldn't handle betrayal well. "At the time I wasn't doing anything illegal, so she'd come to me simply to get to him. Sekijima was like a brother to me. Closer, really, because our bond wasn't random but one we both chose and honored."

Charity was tense as she listened to this story. She hated where she knew it had to be going. Hated that every time it seemed like Daniel had a shot at real happiness, it seemed to elude him. She knew what that felt like. Understood that kind of loneliness in a way she wished she didn't.

"So you turned her over to him?" she asked when he didn't continue. It was the logical thing to assume, but he would have felt torn in two. Having to choose between his loyalty to the man who was like a brother and the woman . . . the woman he'd hoped to build a future with.

She thought about the philosophy that one couldn't move forward without letting go of the past and realized that Daniel was still mired in his past.

"How'd you guess?"

"It was logical. She betrayed you."

He shook his head. "She was only doing her job. I should have . . . but that's in the past."

"What did Sekijima do with her?"

"Well, the government had been pushing hard to infiltrate the Dragon Lords at that time and he had to send a message to them. To let them know that he wasn't going to give any ground."

Daniel reached for a remote in the center console and hit a button. The gates to an underground parking garage parted and he turned neatly into the drive. He waited until the gate closed, making sure that no one had followed them before driving down a ramp and pulling into a vacant parking spot.

"So he killed her?"

"Yes. I tried to think of it as street justice. She knew the risks when she took the assignment. Yuki was Japanese-American, so she knew the kind of men she was dealing with."

But Daniel would still have felt guilty. She had seen it in the way he cared for the people around him. He'd called both his housekeeper and Alonzo from the plane. He didn't look at people as expendable.

That would have been a liability in the life he'd led. She wondered how he'd survived it.

"So you and Sekijima split after her death?"

"No. I understood what he did. But he went after her family, and that I couldn't tolerate."

She reached out to him. He did feel emotions, she thought. They were just so deeply buried. He evaded her touch and she felt like he had slapped her. He wasn't touchy-feely—she knew that—but the rebuff still hurt.

Focus on the job, she thought. Focus. On. The. Job.

She opened her door and scanned the shadows before coming around to Daniel's side. He exited the car and came quickly to her side. They walked together to the elevator station. There was a bare bulb hanging there, making them stand out in the dark, underground garage.

She didn't like it but there wasn't anything she could do about it. She positioned her body behind Daniel's to cover his back. Her microphone was voice-activated and she spoke quickly to her team. "We're in the building. Is the elevator secure?"

"Affirmative," Anna said. "Justine is on her way to meet you."

"Thanks."

"Are we going up now?" Daniel asked, sidestepping her. "Don't put yourself between me and a bullet."

"I'm your bodyguard," she said, blocking him once again. "That's what I'm here for."

She repeated the words to herself because she was sick of

forgetting and treating him like a guy . . . a guy that she wanted and thought could be more in her life.

Daniel heard the footsteps a split second before Charity pushed him against the wall, knocking him off balance. The bullet hit the wall where his head had been a second earlier. She dropped to a crouch and returned fire, but the shooter was impossible to see.

He palmed his Sig Sauer and moved into position. He started to reach for her to get her out of the way, but he realized he'd just get her killed. She needed to concentrate, and he needed to trust that she'd get the job done.

He heard her talking softly, probably alerting Justine of the situation in the garage.

Daniel tuned Charity out and focused on the sounds in the garage, sifting out the ones that were natural and belonged there and finding the ones that would give away the shooter.

He heard the minute scrape of shoe leather against concrete coming from the two spaces left of where he'd parked his car.

Charity touched his arm and nodded in the same direction. She motioned for him to cover her and moved off before he could stop her.

Was there only one shooter in the garage? From past experience he guessed that there would be only one—an assassin to hit him here while the arsonist hit him clear across the country. If it wasn't Sekijima, then the man blackmailing him would have to be one of his brothers. That family knew him very well. And they knew the way he operated.

Having Charity was something they wouldn't expect. The way she looked was the best kind of camouflage for the job she did. But he wasn't taking a chance with her getting injured or killed in the line of duty.

She'd left him in the best position in the garage, protected on three sides by solid walls. One of them housed the elevator, so he'd have to keep an eye on that.

He edged closer to the opening, hearing no sounds. Charity had been wearing boots that looked sexy and lethal at the same time, boots that had a hard heel. He would have expected them to give her away, but her training must have including silent entry.

The elevator door opened behind him and he turned, gun leveled. Justine calmly stepped out and then ducked as the shooter fired two rounds at her head.

"Where's Charity?"

"Out there. Isn't she checking in with you?"

"No. She went silent. Come on."

"Come on?"

"I've got to get you secured and then I'll come back and help her. Not that Charity needs it."

"We're not leaving her," he said.

"Yes, we are. She can draw out the shooter once we know that you are safe."

Daniel hated this, but he had hired Liberty Investigations to protect him. That didn't mean that he had to like it. "I can't leave her out here alone. I know she's highly trained but it goes against the grain. Let's fan out and corner the shooter."

Justine had a hard gaze. Having looked into Charity's gaze, which could be lethal as well, made him realize the difference.

"I'm the boss."

"I'm so sick of hearing that," she said under her breath. "If this backfires, Sam will chew my butt out."

"I'm good."

"You better be."

He didn't say anything, just signaled to her that he'd take the right flank and moved out. He felt the years slip away and the instincts that had kept him alive as a boy flared. He moved with near silence, knowing that the slightest sound would give him away and possibly get him killed.

He was angry that Charity was out there trying to protect him. He knew it was her job, so that wasn't the main source of his rage. It was the fact that he'd shut her out in the car. She'd tried to play it like it didn't matter, but he wouldn't want everything to end between them on this note.

The gun felt like an extension of his arm as he moved through the crowded garage. His eyes had adjusted to the darkness and he stayed low, moving carefully.

Suddenly everything got unnaturally quiet. He felt the minute exhalation of breath on his neck a second before he turned and brought his gun up.

The assailant had a knife which he brought down toward Daniel's neck as he raised his weapon and fired. He hit the man dead center, right between his eyes.

A second bullet ripped through the man's head, and Daniel rolled to the left to miss both the bullet and the knife, which was still coming straight toward him.

He disarmed the dead man, searching for identification in his pockets and finding only the small pin on his collar—the same one that Charity had found earlier.

He glanced up and saw Charity standing in between the cars and the open driveway. Her weapon was held loosely by her side. Justine came up beside her and the two women were like photo negatives of each other.

One blond, the other brunette. Both lethal and vigilant as they watched the garage.

"Was he working alone?" Daniel asked.

"I didn't find anyone else," Justine said.

"Me, either. I drove him this way. What the hell were you thinking?"

Daniel stood up. "Are you talking to me?"

"Yes—and you, Justine," Charity said, turning on her friend. "Our job is to keep him safe. He should be up in that apartment with Anna sitting on top of him, not down here drawing out the assailant."

Justine shrugged. "He handled himself. I'm going to tell Anna to get the police in here."

"I'm taking Daniel upstairs. Send the cops up to get our statements."

Justine nodded and Daniel had a true measure of the reason why Sam Liberty had hired Charity. There was an icy coldness in her eyes but also that fierce protectiveness.

Chapter Thirteen

A man is about as big as the things that make him angry.

—Winston Churchill

Daniel wasn't too into philosophy but figured Winston Churchill knew what he was talking about when it came to anger. He wondered what the leader would say about a woman's anger.

A part of him understood what was going on in Charity's head. He knew that he'd compromised her job by refusing to leave, but he was a man and there was something cowardly about making sure he was safe and secure while his woman—*his woman?*

He followed her through the foyer of his high-rise condo. She was bristling with restless energy—he suspected it was the aftereffects of taking a life. He'd learned a long time ago to process it and move on. His life had been formed by *kill or be killed.*

"Charity?"

"Not yet, Daniel. I'm still likely to say something that will not be nice."

He bit back a smile, something he found himself doing all too often around her. She made him feel good in ways he'd never noticed.

"You're not really mad at me."

She turned to face him, her blond hair flaring out around

her shoulders as she stalked back to him. She had her semi-automatic handgun in her right hand and her left hand was bunched in a fist. As she approached, she lifted her empty hand and punched her index finger at him.

"Hell, yes, I am. Back off. Not another word or else."

"What?"

"Do you realize how incredibly stupid you were in the garage? You could have died—*died!* This isn't a game you're playing, even if Sekijima is treating it like one. Your life is on the line."

She was right in front of him, nose to nose, chest to breasts.

"I'm not going to let some hit man kill me. If Sekijima wants me dead, he's going to have to do the job himself. And I think he knows that, too. He sent that hit man to get you out of the way, Charity."

She shook her head at him. "Don't turn this around. I'm the bodyguard, not you. I take the risks while you are safely tucked away. When I send someone to take you to safety, I expect you to go."

She bit her lower lip, a fine trembling shaking her body. He wrapped his arms around her, drew her tight against him, pressing her face into his shoulder.

She turned her face into his neck and he heard her breathe deeply, felt the exhalation of her breath against his neck. Then her arms came around his waist under his suit jacket, her free hand digging into his skin through the fabric of his shirt.

She clung tightly to him and he let himself believe that she was the only one holding on so tight. But he needed the body contact with her, needed to feel her in his arms now, after he'd come close to losing her.

When had she become important to him?

"It could have been you," she said softly.

He tipped her head up and stared into those gray eyes of hers and felt his world tip on its axis. This woman wasn't his.

She couldn't be his, but man, he wanted her to be. He wanted to stake a claim that the world would see, mark her in the old ways that every man would fear and acknowledge.

But knowing Charity, she'd kick his ass for even thinking such a thing. It was one of the things he really liked about her.

"It could have been you," he said. "I won't let anyone harm you when I can stop them."

"Daniel . . ."

He didn't want to talk anymore. He needed to kiss her. Needed to feel her mouth moving under his so he could really know deep inside that they were both alive. That they were both here together. And his bed was upstairs. He wanted her there. Needed to see her sunshine-blond hair on his pillow so that when she was gone from his life, he'd be able to remember her in his private sanctuary.

His mouth moved over hers with more force than he'd anticipated but he couldn't stop himself. He wrapped his hand in her hair and held her head still. Thrusting his tongue deep, she moaned as he took her mouth. He wrapped his free arm around her waist and lifted her off her feet.

Her legs came up around him and her hands got caught in his suit jacket. He set her on her feet and shrugged out of it, tossing it aside. He needed them both naked, wanted to feel her bare skin pressed against his. He loosened his tie and ripped open the front of his shirt, reaching for her again. She put her gun on the console table next to them.

He pulled her back into his arms. He didn't want to breathe unless the air had been touched by her mouth first. He fisted his hand in her hand, wanting to be gentle. But his feelings were too raw where Charity was concerned. What he really needed was to be buried hilt-deep in her body.

Then maybe the fear that he'd felt for her safety would abate. Maybe then he'd be able to put on his suit jacket and fasten his tie again and go back to pretending he was a civilized man.

Right now, however, he was straight from the cave. All instincts and needs. He unfastened her leather pants and pushed them down her hips. They got caught on her shoes and he let out a growl of frustration. But Charity caged his face in her hands, kissing him with sweet passion.

"Give me a second."

He nodded, reaching for the zipper on her leather jacket and drawing it down while she used the toe of one foot to push off her shoe. He liked her head hitting him mid-chest when she was in her bare feet.

She kicked free of her pants just as he slipped his finger under the cup of her sexy black bra. It wasn't fancy or lacy but it was still sexy as hell against her pale skin.

He pushed the fabric cup of her bra down and bent to capture her beaded nipple between his lips, sucking her deep into his mouth, trying to assuage a thirst that was only for Charity. He felt an ache deep inside where he'd always been alone, something that could only be caused by this woman.

She held him to her and he heard her sigh. Understood that they were more connected in this moment than he'd expected.

He caressed her back and spine, scraping his nail down the length of it. He followed the straps of her bra around to the front and felt her through the silk of her undergarment.

She closed her eyes and held her breath as he fondled her through the material. Peeling back the cup, he ran his finger over her nipple. It was velvety compared to the satin smoothness of her breast. He brushed his finger back and forth until she bit her lower lip and shifted under his touch. She was so alive. So damned alive right this moment, when she'd been so close to dying in the garage.

Her sweet moan drew him back to her body. He leaned down and licked at her lips until she tipped her head to the side and allowed him access to her mouth.

He lifted her by the waist and she wrapped her legs around him, rubbing her center over his erection.

God, he hadn't been this hot since . . . he couldn't remember ever being this hot for a woman. He scraped his fingernail over her nipple and she shivered in his arms. He pushed the cup of her bra off of her breast. Glancing down at her bare flesh, he saw the nipple distended and begging for his mouth. He lowered his head and suckled.

He held her still with a hand on the small of her back. He buried his other hand in her hair and arched her over his arm so that both breasts were thrust up at him. He had his arms full of woman—a woman he wanted more than any other.

Her eyes were closed, her hips moving subtly against him, and when he blew on her nipple he saw gooseflesh spread down her body.

He pushed the fabric from her other breast and bent to suckle her some more. He loved the way she reacted to his mouth on her breasts. Her nipples were so sensitive, he was pretty sure he could bring her to an orgasm just from touching her there.

The globes of her breasts were full and fleshy, more than a handful. He hardened as he wondered what his cock would feel like thrust between them.

He leaned down and licked the valley between her breasts, imagining his cock sliding back and forth there. He'd swell and she'd moan his name watching him.

He bit carefully at the lily-white skin of her chest, suckling at her so he'd leave his mark. Hell, he wanted to tattoo his name on her so that any man who saw her would know she was his. Possessiveness was foreign to him, but with this woman he felt the need to stake a claim.

But that was out of the question, so instead he sucked hard at her skin, not lifting his head until he was sure he'd left his mark on her. He wanted her to remember this moment and what they had done when she was alone later.

He kept kissing and rubbing, pinching her nipples until her hands clenched in his hair and she rocked her hips harder against his length. He lifted his hip, thrusting up against her and then biting carefully on her tender, aroused nipple. She screamed his name and he hurriedly covered her mouth with his.

Rocking her until the storm passed and she quieted in his arms, he held her close, her bare breasts brushing against his shirt front. He was so hard he thought he'd die if he didn't free himself and get inside her.

He held her in his arms, his erection still between them. She smiled up at him and he felt a clenching deep inside him.

Daniel carried her down the hall and into his bedroom. He closed the door with his heel and then walked over to the bed, then set her on her feet.

She knew that sex right now would be about adrenaline but she didn't care. She needed him in her body. Needed more than just an orgasm to feel like he was really safe.

She'd never been scared for a client the way she'd been about Daniel in the garage. It was the first time she hadn't been able to shut her mind down and just concentrate on doing her job. As much as she knew she needed to check in with Anna and discuss the man they'd killed in the garage, she really just wanted this. Needed to feel Daniel's arms wrapped around her, his body buried inside her.

She'd never expected the pleasure she experienced with him to be like this. "Finish getting undressed and lie on the bed."

He was too bossy, but she felt a little tingle of excitement at his orders. "Only if you take yours off, too."

"Ladies first."

She shook her head, but pushed her jacket off and finished removing her bra. She put her hands on her hips. "Your turn."

"On the bed," he said.

"Are you going to be stubborn about this?"

"Hell, yeah."

She pivoted really slowly and then walked to the bed, using her runway experience from her modeling days. She moved slowly, sensuously—deliberately trying to entice him with every step she took.

"Charity." He said her name but it came out as a growl.

She stopped, looking back over her shoulder. "Yes?"

"Get on the bed before I take you against the wall."

She licked her lips and blew him a kiss. "I might let you."

He lunged toward her, but she wasn't ready to stop playing with him yet. She dove for the bed, doing a neat tuck and roll that left her lying in the exact center of the king-sized mattress. "Was this what you wanted?"

"Yes."

He sank down on the edge of the bed. Leaning over her, he lowered his mouth to hers. His kisses overwhelmed her. She'd never felt this kind of burning desire before. All she wanted to do was make love to him She should be thinking about Sekijima and saving his skin, but they were safe here. She knew Anna and Justine had her back and she also knew once she left this bedroom, their intimacy would end.

The way he'd acted in the garage was a warning. She was going to have to force him to be safe, and that was going to make intimacy . . . impossible. She pulled back, looking up at him, wanting to memorize his face so that later when she was alone she'd be able to remember this.

She brought her hand up between her breasts and fingered the hickey he'd left on her chest. He brushed her fingers aside, rubbing his mangled forefinger over it. "I should apologize for marring your skin."

"But?"

"I wanted to mark you as mine."

"Oh, Daniel," she said, because there were no other words to say.

He cupped her face and lowered his head to hers, as he thrust his tongue deep in her mouth. She felt the rekindling of her own desire. She wanted him again. She tried to angle her head to reciprocate, but he held her still.

She felt a fierce need in him to dominate her, to remind her that she was his. She found the proof she was searching for that Daniel was different from every other man she'd ever met.

Her nipples tightened and her breasts felt too full as he pulled her into his embrace. He canted his hips toward hers, the ridge of his erection bumping against her. She moaned deep in her throat and clung to him.

His biceps flexed as he shifted her in his arms, rolling her under his body. Running his hands over her body.

His mouth moved down the column of her neck, nibbling and biting softly. He lingered at the base of her neck where she knew her pulse beat frantically. Then he sucked on her skin. Everything in her body clenched. Not enough to push her over the edge, just enough to make her hungry—frantic for more of him.

She scored his shoulders with her fingernails, felt the fine linen fabric of his shirt. She pushed it off his shoulders, taking her time to unfasten the cuff links and put them on the nightstand; then she pushed the shirt off of his shoulders.

As soon as she saw his arms she knew why he'd kept his shirt on the first time they'd made love. His arms were covered in the beautiful ritual tattoos of the Yakuza.

She knew if she asked him anything, he'd shut her down, so she tugged him onto the bed next to her and got up on her knees. She traced the design up his left arm and then crawled around behind his back to trace the large dragon there.

"This creature looks so fierce, so dangerous."

He pulled her around onto his lap. "Remember that I am, too."

"Yes, you are," she said, pushing him back toward the pillows. She skimmed her hands down his chest. Tucked his loosened pants down his legs. She removed his shoes and socks and then took care of all his clothes. When he was naked, she lowered herself over his body. The full contact of flesh to flesh was exquisite.

She sighed at the rightness of it as he rolled her body under his. She caressed his flat male nipples as he held himself above her on his strong arms. She liked the way she was surrounded by him, felt very feminine as she lay there under him. His skin was hot to the touch and she wrapped her arms around his body, pulling him closer.

He pulled back, staring down at her. Then he traced one finger over the full globes of her breasts. She shifted her shoulders, waiting for his caress. He took one of her nipples between his thumb and forefinger, pinching lightly.

She shook with need, unable to wait for him.

She reached between their bodies, but he shifted his hips out of her reach. His mouth fastened on her left nipple, suckling her strongly. She undulated against him, her hips lifting toward him. He drew his other hand down her body, his fingers tangling in the hair at her center.

He caressed her between her legs until she was frantically holding his head to her breasts, trying to find her release, but it remained just out of her reach. She skimmed her hands down his body, caressing his hip bone, and then moving her fingers around to his cock.

His breath hissed out as she reached between his legs to cup his sac and caress his length.

"There's a condom in the nightstand."

"I'm on the pill," she said, too busy exploring him to really pay attention to what he said. But she did pay attention to the way his breath caught whenever she scored his sac with her nails.

"I haven't always been careful," he said, shifting over her, opening the nightstand drawer and pulling out a condom. He tossed it on her stomach.

"Put it on me."

"With pleasure."

She placed it on his tip and then rolled it down his hard

length. He groaned deep in his throat. She started to reach lower again, but he caught her hand and stretched it over her head. He lifted her leg up around his hip.

She felt him hot, hard, and ready at her entrance, but he made no move to take her. She looked up at him.

"Watch me take you, Charity, and know that this means that you belong to me."

He thrust inside her then, lifting her up, holding her with his big hands as he repeatedly drove into her. He went deeper than he had earlier. She felt completely full, stretched and surrounded by him.

He bit her neck carefully and sucked against her skin. She suspected he was marking her as his, because he'd looked up at her before deliberately drawing on her skin. She wanted to do the same to him. To show the world that this man was hers.

Everything tightened inside her until she felt her climax spread through her body. Her skin was pulsing, her body tightening around his plunging cock. A minute later, he came, crying her name and holding her tightly to his chest.

She rested her head on his shoulder and held him. Wrapped completely around his body, she realized the truth of what he'd said. She *was* his. She knew he meant temporarily, but it felt permanent and she'd spent her entire life afraid of permanency. Afraid of being this close to one person because she knew how fragile life was. She knew that it took one careless act to take someone from this life.

And Daniel was playing a very dangerous game, one that she wasn't too sure she could keep him safe in. That was what really scared her. Not Sekijima or the people he sent after Daniel, but the fact that Daniel didn't care who was sent after him. He wasn't going to hide and stay safe.

Chapter Fourteen

I believe that uncertainty is really my spirit's way of whispering, "I'm in flux. Something's off-balance here."
—Oprah Winfrey

Charity knew something was off-balance in her life, and she suspected it was herself. She showered in one of the guest bathrooms in Daniel's luxury apartment. Anna had knocked on the bedroom door, handed Charity her pants, and then said she needed to see her in fifteen minutes.

It should have been embarrassing but somehow hadn't been. Instead, Daniel had offered her his bathrobe and directed her to this bathroom.

She soaped her body, lingering over the hickey he'd left between her breasts. Her body ached from his possession and she felt in flux, as if she was between the woman she'd been her entire adult life and a new woman she was meant to become.

It was dangerous, this crazy feeling that she experienced whenever she was around Daniel, because she needed to be completely in control. She wrapped her arms around her waist and sank down against the marble wall of the shower. The water washed over her, and, for a brief second, she let herself go. Let herself believe that she was falling in love with Daniel. Let her mind's eye remember the beauty of those Yakuza tattoos down his arms and back.

And she refused at this moment to dwell on their significance. On the fact that she was going to have to force Daniel to come clean about his past. And admit to being in the Dragon Lords.

The Dragon Lords were dangerous and far-reaching. For the first time since she'd taken the assignment to protect Daniel, she had some real fear that she might not be able to keep him safe. Until that moment when she'd seen his back, she'd thought there wasn't any enemy of his that she couldn't protect him from.

But now Sekijima's actions took on a new significance: he was sending his assassin squad after Daniel, hoping to take him completely out of this world.

That sobering thought was enough to tinge the happiness she'd felt a few seconds ago. There was no happy-ever-after. Hell, she knew that. She wasn't the type to buy into fairy tales. Even as a little girl she hadn't really wanted a white knight to save her. She'd always imagined saving him.

She turned off the shower and toweled dry, refusing to look at herself in the mirror, not wanting to confront herself and see something in her eyes she didn't want to accept.

She dressed carefully in a clean pair of leather pants. She hated the way they chafed when she sweated, but leather offered more protection than any other material. And the pants were subtle and moved with her skin. Plus, these pants had built-in pockets for all the weapons she liked to carry. She put on a cotton T-shirt and tucked it into the pants, then put on her shoulder holster with the Sig Sauer she always carried.

At the small of her back she fastened a second gun, this one a small pistol. She added a thin throwing dagger next to the gun, then put her earpiece microphone in and listened to the conversations of her friends.

They were discussing the case and she knew when she left the bathroom she had to stop acting like . . . well, like such a girl. She needed to be focused and all business. There would be no more little dalliances like the one she'd just had with Daniel.

She had an ankle sheath for another knife and one she strapped onto her thigh. She was as armed as she could be, but she had the fear that there weren't enough weapons to protect Daniel if he was determined to draw Sekijima out.

She pulled her hair back into a ponytail so it would be out of her face and then put on her shoes. Ready as she'd ever be, she left the bathroom, following the sound of the voices.

Anna, Justine, and Daniel were all sitting in the living room. Everyone looked up as she walked in—she hated the silence as they watched her. "Catch me up on what's going on," she said.

Justine raised one eyebrow. "The cops will be here in about fifteen minutes to take your statement. I had to bring Sam into it—he's forwarded the threats Daniel received in D.C. The local cops offered to assign someone to watch this place."

"I've declined," Daniel said. "The fewer people involved, the better. Sekijima has proved he's not afraid to strike down anyone around me."

"True," Charity said, "and we're enough protection."

"You're certainly armed for it," Daniel said. "If you'd come into my suite looking like this, I would never have doubted your skills."

"Is that a compliment?" she asked.

"If you want it to be."

There was an edge to every word he uttered, and she had to wonder what was going on in his head. Some men were easy to read, but Daniel was always closed to her. She had no idea what he thought or what motivated him.

She shrugged. "This place actually wouldn't be too bad to secure if you want to set up here to draw Sekijima out."

"I've got a message in to Sam."

"About?"

"You ladies going back to D.C. I'm changing the focus of

your work for me. I just want you to do some research and provide a location for Sekijima if you can find it. No more bodyguard work."

"Why would you do that?"

"Because as you said, Sekijima isn't afraid to take down
everyone around me."

"You can't protect us now," Charity said.

"The hell I can't."

The time away from Charity, even for just those few minutes, had reinforced his need to protect her. He'd worked with
women before, so he knew his motivation wasn't her gender.

It was those clear gray eyes. Those eyes that looked out of
her face, so fierce and determined to catch Sekijima. Those
eyes warned him that if she were caught, she would give nothing away.

Sekijima would revel in that—he'd torture her and Daniel
would go berserk. He'd been concentrating on focusing his
anger on Sekijima, but if something happened to Charity, he
knew he'd take out all of Seattle and everyone from here to
Vancouver.

"Enough of this jerking us back and forth. You're the boss,
we're on the job, and that's the end of it," Justine said.

"Call Sam if you want to, but we're too deeply involved to
pull back now," Charity added.

"Don't be fooled because we're girls," Anna said. "You're
looking at the best in the business."

Daniel wanted to groan inside where no one could hear it.
"I'm not jerking you around."

"I know," Charity said. "I . . . I want you to consider letting
us use a decoy for you. We'll keep you safely tucked away."

A decoy. Never. He ran from no one and nothing. He shook
his head.

"Then we'd better listen to Anna's plan, because it looks
like we're all staying here."

He listened to the women talk and look over the plans for his San Juan home. But he knew he needed to draw back, and that if he had any chance of protecting Charity and her friends, he needed to distance himself from them.

And he also knew that Sekijima wasn't going to give them time to set up anything. Daniel knew his old friend wanted him dead—now. The man was striking at him in increasingly frequent intervals.

"Daniel?

"What?"

"Anna asked if you had the plans for the house."

"Yes. They are in my study."

"Will you get them?"

He nodded and pivoted on his heel, stalking down the hall. His mind was frantically racing over the possibilities. He had an old number . . . the phone was at Sekijima's older brother's house. Von had been injured in a car crash as a boy and the once-powerful Gashira Hosa had been paralyzed.

That action had driven both Daniel and Sekijima to revenge and, eventually, up the ladder in the Dragon Lords. Daniel rubbed the back of his neck as he stared out the floor-to-ceiling glass windows. The skyline of Seattle, with the glittering water of the bay, was spread out before him.

He'd always felt so powerful and proud when he'd stood here. Always felt very much a man in charge of his own destiny. But today he'd realized he was still a pawn. Still not the Oyabun of his own life. And it was time to wrest power back.

Time to find his way back into a life that he'd always thought he had. One where he walked alone.

"Did you find them?"

He glanced over his shoulder as Charity entered. She was wearing leather again, and he knew he was developing a fetish for seeing her long, sexy legs encased in that fabric. This weakness, this out-of-control feeling, was exactly why he needed to get away from her.

"Not yet."

She came into his study and closed the richly colored, walnut-paneled door behind her. Her boot heels made a muted sound against the carpet.

"Where did you learn to walk like that?" he asked, the words torn out of his throat. She moved like a wet dream. All sensuous gliding. Her shoulders back, breasts thrust forward, hips rolling.

"On the catwalk . . . you like it?"

"I'd have to be dead not to."

She nodded. "You give nothing away."

"It's how I've stayed alive for so long."

She walked around the perimeter of the room, stopping beneath the portrait that he'd had commissioned to go on the wall. It was in the style of the old Japanese master. Large, dominant, and full of fantasy images, it captured for Daniel a feeling of the past.

It reminded him of the old days, and that kept him on his toes, usually. Seeing Charity standing in front of it just reminded him that he wanted her. For the first time he thought of the future in terms as something other than survival.

With Charity he longed to be a different man. The kind who would plant his seed in her belly and then watch her grow with his child. The type who'd build her a big mansion that she could live in and then live there with her. The type who . . . didn't have a death sentence hanging over him.

"Daniel?"

"Yes?"

"You are staring at me and I don't think it's a good thing."

Fuck. She messed with his head . . . "It's all good. Your walk is definitely not something that a bodyguard should be able to do."

"Why is that?"

"Because it brings men to their knees."

She walked over to the large Japanese wood desk and hopped up on the surface. "Will it work with Sekijima?"

Daniel shook his head. "He'd let you believe it was working right up until he slipped a blade between your ribs."

Her eyes widened but she didn't show any fear. "He's not going to compromise?"

"Not at all. He won't stop until he has me and he'll use anyone to that end."

Charity watched Daniel carefully. She'd let him hide things about his past, but no more. When he'd left the room, she'd mentioned to the other women that Daniel had once been in the Yakuza, that he bore the traditional tattooing of a gang member.

Then Anna had started researching him, stumbling onto something that shocked all three of them. Daniel had paid a blackmailer off once before. There on the page it was hard to get all of the details, but the end result was clear. Despite his legitimate business interests, Daniel had definitely done some illegal things.

Things he'd been fined for and warned that jail time was an option if he didn't clean up his act.

Charity realized that she didn't know Daniel. She'd thought him a man of honor, a man who lived by his own moral compass, and it had been shocking to find out that wasn't so.

"Why won't Sekijima stop?"

"It's just not a concept he understands," Daniel said.

"What about you? Do you understand stopping?"

He walked over to her, coming right up to where she sat on his desk. He put his hands on either side of her hips and stepped forward until his thighs brushed against her dangling legs.

"Not with you."

"Don't, Daniel. Every time you touch me I forget something important."

"What's that?" he asked. His hands grasped her hips and she closed her eyes for a second.

This close to him, it was impossible not to feel surrounded. The warmth of his body, the minty freshness of his breath, the scent of his expensive aftershave . . .

"That you're not the man I think you are," she said, forcing her mind to stay focused. "That you are hiding something from me."

"You know all my secrets now," he said. "You've seen my tattoos, the scarlet letter that stains my skin from my past."

God, she ached for him. Even now, even knowing he wasn't the man she thought he was, she still ached to comfort him. To find a way to make a life with him.

But he was a man who walked on both sides of the law and she was firmly on one side only. On the side of all law-abiding citizens, and it was something she refused to compromise.

"If it were just a stain, you would have moved on," she said the words softly but they echoed in the room. Echoed in the space that slowly developed between them as he stepped away from her.

"What are you saying?"

"Anna's uncovered something in your past . . . another blackmail attempt." She chose her words carefully because she had wanted to hear the story from him and not make him reveal it because they'd find out another way.

He shook his head, cursing succinctly under his breath. "How did she find out about that?"

"There's nothing we can't find out when we start working a case. That's why we're so good." She wanted to grab him by the shoulders and force him to answer the damn questions. Tell her the fricking truth for once.

"That really has nothing to do with what's happening today. Leave that alone."

"That? Can't you be more specific?" she asked, unwilling to let this go.

"Yes, but I won't be. I didn't give you carte blanche to poke around in my life. There are things in my past—incidents, if you will—that are better left there. Things even I don't want to remember, much less have someone like you know about them." Daniel ran his hands through his hair, ruffling his civilized image.

She didn't understand him. She knew that protecting her had somehow become important to him, or was that simply a ruse he was using to keep her at bay? Dammit, was she really going to fall for another man who didn't see her for who she was? How many times did she have to learn that lesson?

She wasn't stupid, she reminded herself. But when it came to the men she fell for, she felt like an idiot sometimes.

"We're not going to stop digging. This threat from Sekijima is too dangerous and without full knowledge of why he's after you . . . we might make a mistake."

Daniel stalked away, back to the floor-to-ceiling windows, where he placed his hands against the glass and leaned forward.

"What do you want from me?" he asked at last, his gaze meeting hers. She felt that maybe this time he'd come clean.

"The truth," she said.

She didn't even have to think about it. "I can't trust you without it."

"Some things . . . I've done things that you won't approve of." There was no shame in his voice, only a type of resignation. He knew he didn't have the answers she needed, but he was willing to try to give them to her.

"My approval isn't important," she said. "Your safety is."

"I . . . I paid the blackmail the first time because I didn't want to lose all of this," he said, gesturing not only to the room but the city skyline as well.

"Was this before Yuki?" she asked.

"Yes. Long before her."

She hopped off the desk and walked over to him when she realized he wasn't going to turn and face her. She bent down and slipped under his arms so she had her back to the window.

She put her hands on his shoulders and pushed him back away from all that glass.

"You can't stand in front of a window like this."

"The glass is bulletproof."

That revealed so much about the kind of life he led. And it fit with everything she was coming to know about him. Daniel hadn't lived an easy life. He had to constantly be on guard. Constantly be waiting for a threat from his past to come and take away all he'd worked so hard for.

"I need to know about the other blackmailer . . . the one you paid off. Maybe this new threat is connected to that in some way."

Daniel walked over to the wet bar and poured himself two fingers of good Scotch whiskey. He downed it in a single swallow and then looked back at her.

His eyes, which were usually so blank, so devoid of any emotion, seemed filled with anger.

"The blackmailer I paid off before was Sekijima. It's totally connected to him and to my past."

"Is he using the same thing to threaten you this time?" she asked. "What is that, by the way?"

"Not really the exact same thing."

"What did he use the first time?"

"He used my past. The illegal things I'd done to climb my way up in the Dragon Lords. He threatened to make those actions public."

"How? It's not like it would have been safe for him to go to the cops," Charity said.

"He had photos of the crimes I'd committed."

"What kind of crimes?" she asked, almost afraid to hear the answer.

"Murder."

"What?"

"I was Sekijima's hit man."

Chapter Fifteen

Forget injuries, never forget kindness.
                                        —Confucius

Daniel's life had been filled with injuries and it had shaped the man he was. He knew the wisdom of Confucius and had spent some time trying to make sense of his life when he'd battled back from the blackmail. How was he going to explain that to Charity?

For him the odd part was that he actually wanted to. And he saw the horror on her face when he'd said the words hit man, but he wasn't going to hide anymore. Sam's ladies were digging up information that he assumed would never see the light of day. In fact, it hadn't until now.

"Hit man?"

He struggled not to just say the hell with this and walk away. But having held Charity in his arms, having come so close to tasting the one thing that had always been out of his reach—true peace and happiness—he had to try.

"Um . . . yeah, I've always had an affinity for weapons."

"Well, so have I but I don't kill unless I have to."

He shook his head. "Charity, I had to. It was the only way to move up in the Yakuza. I had no ties to anyone. No family, until the Dragon Lords."

She just continued to watch him, her eyes wide. Which made him want to keep talking to her, as if he could somehow wipe away the stain of the past by explaining himself and then somehow . . . what? She'd forgive him? Did he really need her forgiveness? Hell, no, but he wanted her understanding.

He didn't want her to look at him and see a monster.

"And your family demanded that you kill?" she asked, her voice quiet and flat.

"Yes. It was the one thing I was good at. I slept with a knife and attacked more than one member if they got too close to me." God, he wasn't going to tell her this. Tell her about Bo Long, the boy who'd watched him with envy and a lust to kill him. He had to keep his damned mouth shut. There were things that she could never know. Like how he'd been an amoral killer. He hadn't ever been overly emotional about killing—well, it had become his job. Leaving that world behind, moving into the corporate life, had been harder than many would have believed. But he'd done it.

He'd made a break with that part of himself, yet when the Dragon Lords had called him he'd always gone back. One more time. One last job. One last chance to pay back the debt he'd owed to Sekijima and his family for giving him a roof over his head.

"Sekijima threatened to leak photos of the men you killed to the press?"

Sort of. "Yes."

"How much did it cost you to keep paying off the blackmail? How long did it last?"

The cost was one she'd never understand. Sekijima hadn't wanted money. The man was wealthy and powerful. What he'd wanted was for Daniel—his best hit man—to come out of retirement. Sekijima had used his leverage three times after Daniel tried to leave his life as a Dragon Lord. And three times he'd answered the call.

He let himself believe that he did it because he owed another man a debt. Never admitting he did it because . . . well, because deep inside he knew that was the man he really was.

He knew that the corporate world he'd started to move in was really nothing more than a fresh coat of paint on the rusted-out hull of the man he'd always been.

"Daniel?"

"It wasn't money he wanted. And he came to me three times before I finally put a stop to it."

"What did he want?"

"For me to keep working for him."

"Did you?"

"What do you think? Didn't Anna find something that said I'd paid off my blackmailer before?"

Charity came closer to him and he struggled to hold his ground. When he was in the past, he felt dirtied by it, knew there was no way he'd ever be the man he liked to pretend he was now. Staring down into her beautiful face, he knew he wasn't the man she needed. That he never could be, and that pissed him off.

"Yes, we did find that. So what happened? You stopped paying the blackmail, right?"

Daniel knew she wasn't naïve. He'd seen her run down an assassin and she'd calmly shot the man that Sekijima had sent after them in the garage. But she'd done it for a noble cause. She'd done it because she wanted to protect him.

"If I tell you . . ."

"Trust me, Daniel. I'll keep your secrets safe. I'm not about to tell anyone what you've revealed. But I can't really protect you if I don't know what we're up against."

He reached for her. Touched the side of her face with that mangled forefinger of his, then cupped her jaw and tipped her head back. He leaned down, brushing his lips over hers lightly. He wanted her to remember he wasn't just the hard Yakuza. He wanted her to somehow remember that he was more than that with her. That with her he had the potential to be her man.

She wrapped her arms around his waist and pulled him

close to her body. She felt so small next to his bulky muscles. But as he skimmed his free hand down her back, he felt the sheath with the gun and the knife.

He felt a twinge of arousal shoot down his spine, pooling at his groin. He groaned. Why did everything about her turn him on?

Finally she pulled away. Stepped back and waited for him to continue telling her about his past.

The truth hit him in a rush. He never looked to the past, not because he'd moved on but because he didn't want to remember.

What he'd been trying to forget was he hadn't hated that old life, and this new one wasn't as fulfilling as he'd always thought it would be. But finally seeing Charity standing in his study, he thought he found a reason to let it go.

Charity struggled with all the things that Daniel revealed to her. She'd had an idea that his life wasn't all that great because of the things he'd already told her about his past. But this new information . . . she didn't know how to make it fit with the man she'd come to know.

A man who cared not only about the corporation he ran, but who also really cared about his staff. She'd met hit men before. She'd seen cold-blooded killers and knew that they'd somehow managed to find a way to take the humanity out of the equation. Their humanity.

Something she'd never been able to do. She'd always struggled with the very necessary job of killing. Even Kenkichi, who had fueled her own rage and been responsible for leading her to the path that had brought her here. She'd thrown up after she'd killed him. She hadn't realized that she was never going to find peace in meting out justice.

It had taken another person's outrage to lead her away from her own remorse and guilt at being Kenkichi's executioner. His face still haunted her to this day.

She wondered if there were any faces that did that to Daniel. Was there any part of him that regretted what he'd become?

"You were going to tell me how you stopped being blackmailed."

He put his arms behind his back, the motion pulling the fabric of his dress shirt taut against his skin. As she remembered the smoothness of his body, electric tingles spread over her and she turned away from him. Lust. Why did it have to be lust now when she needed her synapses firing on all fronts?

"I had to remove the threat to stop the blackmail."

"The threat was Sekijima," she said, thinking out loud, putting it together with what he'd said about thinking the other man was dead. "You killed him."

"Tried to. I got his inner guard and he was lying in a pool of blood when I walked away."

She gasped at the image and he stopped talking. She'd asked for his secrets and she knew that now she had to prove she was worthy of keeping them.

"Sorry. It's just that I know you thought of him as your brother. That must have been a difficult choice."

Daniel shook his head. "We lived by a code, Sekijima and I. That code was one where black and white were absolute."

"I guess it would have to be, considering the life you led. How did he cross the line? Was it when Yuki was killed?"

He shook his head. "No. Not at all. That I understood. She'd made the reckless decision to try to infiltrate the Dragon Lords."

"Then what was it? What line did he cross?"

"He refused to honor our bargain. I paid his price and he gave his word to let those photos go. And in the end he wasn't going to stop. He knew it and I knew it."

"But he was your brother."

"Not when he started using me. We'd always had honor between us. We worked together to move up in the Dragon Lords. Though I feel Japanese in my soul, I knew that I'd never have the position of Oyabun and so did Sekijima."

"Was that something you would have wanted?" she asked.

"In another life, perhaps. But now, I don't think so."

"You both worked together to make him the Oyabun, didn't you?"

"Yes. Once he achieved the position of power he repaid me by asking me to take over one of the legitimate businesses of the Yakuza. An import/export shipping company. I agreed and started using my power. I cleaned up my image as a street hood, did what it took to make the legit business really work."

They'd both gotten what they'd always wanted, and she could tell from what he said that the success he'd achieved hadn't given him what he'd been searching for. She wondered if he even knew what he'd wanted.

"What happened then?"

"Everything was good for a few years, and then the incident with Yuki. After that I broke ties with the Dragon Lords. Another faction moved against Sekijima and he needed a man he could trust to go after their leader.

"He came to me, and I did the job for him, never suspecting that he was setting me up. The photos came from that job."

Charity's heart ached for him. To Daniel, loyalty was so very important, and he'd honored that old bond with Sekijima by doing him a favor and he'd been betrayed. Could he ever really trust again? She didn't think so. The one man he'd always had confidence in had done the unthinkable.

"A few weeks after that he starting blackmailing me. He was no longer my friend but a powerful Oyabun who demanded my fidelity."

"But you no longer felt bound to him."

"You're right. I didn't. That's when he showed me the photos and the video surveillance. I would have gone to jail for murder."

"Why didn't you take out the surveillance cameras?"

Daniel gave her a really hard look and she almost backed

down, but he wasn't a stupid man and that kind of mistake was too careless for him.

"My spotter was supposed to take care of that."

Now it all made sense. "I'm not sure what Sekijima's motivation is in all this now. You're not going to be his hit man—he must know that."

"Yes, he knows that."

Scenarios were spinning in her mind, like puzzle pieces that she couldn't make fit. She kept on working it from every angle, and then they started falling into place.

"Blackmail's not his true goal in all this, is it?"

Daniel just watched with that level green stare of his.

"He's going to leave you for dead."

"Exactly."

Daniel had expected fear or revulsion from Charity but instead she took on a steely-eyed look.

"I'm not going to let that happen, Daniel."

"Sweetheart, I don't know that you can stop him."

"I do." She nibbled her lower lip and then tipped her head to one side. "You called me sweetheart."

"That's right, I did."

"Did you mean it?"

"Yes."

"I . . . I know this is a crazy time for you."

"You, too," he said, walking slowly toward her. "But?"

"I . . . I'm not sure what I was going to say," she said.

He knew that she had chickened out. It surprised him because she was so brave about everything.

"I never figured you for a coward."

"Don't make me get tough with you," she said, a teasing note in her voice and in her eyes.

He wanted to tease her some more. Draw her out of the sadness and lethal intensity that had swamped her when he was telling her of his past.

"I'm not afraid of you, Charity."

"Good."

"Are you?" he asked, needing to know if what he'd revealed had finally pushed her away, had finally shown her that he was less than the man she deserved. He wouldn't apologize for who he was; otherwise, his entire life would have no meaning, and he'd learned a long time ago to live with himself.

"Afraid of myself?" she asked. "Not at all."

He shook his head. "I never figured you for obtuse."

"I'm not afraid of you, Daniel. There are things you said that scare me, but if I start talking about them, I'm fearful I'll lose my focus. And right now, protecting you is more important than dealing with my emotions."

He couldn't stop himself from going over to her. She looked like a badass in her black clothing with all those weapons, but her eyes were soft and sad. Sad for him, he thought. Sad for the brother he'd lost when Sekijima betrayed him.

No one had ever cared about him that way. Even he wasn't sure that he cared about the loss of Sekijima. A part of him refused to acknowledge the pain of losing that relationship. The Yakuza had been his family for so long and when he'd left . . . he'd been all alone.

"Sweetheart," he said, drawing her into his arms, sweeping his hands down her back to linger on her backside. He cupped her and drew her into the curve of his body.

But she wedged her hands between their bodies and pushed him away. He let her go because he had no idea how to handle this situation.

"I meant it. Once I go emotional . . . Just don't do that right now," Charity said.

"I want to comfort you." And he did. He wanted to be her rock. And he'd never been there for anyone before, never gave a fuck about what anyone else felt or if they were upset by his actions. But with Charity—all bets were off.

She glanced down at the front of his pants where his erection strained. "That doesn't look like comfort."

She startled a laugh out of him. He was shocked because he always guarded his responses. He hadn't laughed—ever. His life just wasn't given to frivolity. And the situation they were in, where death was stalking them—well, he hadn't expected it.

She smiled then. "I like your laugh."

He just shook his head and walked over to her, cupped her face in his hands and tilted her head back until he was looking down into her gray eyes. There was strength in them, caring in them. And he relished being the man she felt those things for.

"I'll take sex if you don't want comfort."

She flushed a little and licked her lips. He groaned at the sight of her sweet pink tongue moving over her lips. "Not now. The cops will be here any minute to take our statements. And if Anna interrupts us again, I'll die of embarrassment."

"I won't." He caught her around the waist and drew her back into the curve of his body. She rested against him for a minute, her arms wrapping around him and squeezing him tight.

"Of course you won't—you're a man." She stepped away from him and ran her finger down the center of his body, stopping at his belt. His erection pulsed and he canted his hips forward.

She caressed him briefly and then stepped back. He almost groaned out loud at the loss of her touch.

"Is that supposed to be a compliment or an insult?" he asked, forcing his thoughts away from his groin.

"Just a statement of fact," she said, turning and walking to the door. "Did you find the plans for your San Juan home?"

"No. Sekijima is never going to wait for me to go out there to attack. He's probably already working his way into the highrise here."

"Why didn't you say this before? I was going to send you away. Or lock you in my command center. It's impenetrable."

"Hide me away?" he asked. Never. He didn't hide. He fought and challenged his enemies. He could never hide while a woman went out and risked her life for him.

"I want to protect you, Charity."

"Why? You know I can handle myself."

"You're the only thing I've had that I want to keep and I'm not going to let Sekijima get you."

He had no right to that thought or desire but it was what he felt. His entire focus had changed sometime during the day. Getting to Sekijima and finishing their blood feud was no longer the most important objective in this game. Protecting Charity was, and he knew he was damned good at achieving objectives when he set his mind to them.

"I'm not going to let him get me *or* you. Together we are going to stop him."

Together. Even with Sekijima, he'd essentially been alone. That was how the Yakuza ran. Though they did work toward a common goal, most of them operated through their own networks. In Japan there was more of a sense of openness about being in the Yakuza, but here in the U.S. it was different.

"I'm not much of a team player."

"Good thing you're a quick learner," she said.

"What makes you think I am?" he asked, following her out of the study and down the hall to the living room where her friends waited.

"Just following a hunch."

"A hunch? That's not what I'm paying for."

"Haven't you ever heard of woman's intuition?" she asked.

"Yeah, but I think I'd take a Glock at my side over intuition."

"In this case you get both. Except I carry a Sig Sauer."

"And handle it with amazing skill."

"That's high praise coming from you," she said as they entered the room where her friends waited.

The cops were waiting as well, which is the only reason why he didn't pull her back into his arms and kiss her sassy mouth.

Chapter Sixteen

Only I can change my life. No one can do it for me.
                                                —Andy Warhol

Daniel had been set on a certain path since he'd broken with the Dragon Lords. Yet a part of him had stayed mired there. It was hard to go from living one way—by the Yakuza rules, where he'd been revered and feared—to the corporate world where he was respected, but only to some extent.

Over the years he'd learned a different way to function but a part of him—the raw, rough street punk—still longed for the days when he could pull out his gun or knife and settle differences without playing games.

He was on edge and didn't really enjoy the function nearly as much as he should have. The charity dinner was one he'd been committed to attending more than three months earlier. Having Charity on his arm, dressed in a one-of-a-kind designer gown, was, well, not a hardship.

"Remind me again why you are here," Charity said. She hadn't wanted to come to this function. She thought there were too many variables. The Liberty Investigations team had tried and failed to vet the attendee list for anyone who worked for Sekijima.

Daniel knew they wouldn't find a reference, yet at the same time he knew that Sekijima would send someone here. And

Daniel planned to use that person to lead him back to his old enemy. And end things.

"Because I gave my word that I'd attend. You're just angry I made you leave the knife in the car."

"That and the fact that you wouldn't wear the Kevlar vest under your tux." She rested her hand in the curve of his arm.

To the world, he wondered, did they look like just another couple at a corporate event? "This is too public a place. Trust me. Sekijima will come after me when it's just the two of us."

"Is that why we left the apartment empty? I don't like that idea."

"I'm well aware of all of your arguments." She'd been firm in her views and hadn't backed down from her arguments. He liked that about her. She stated her point of view with facts, not using emotion or manipulation to get what she wanted like women he'd known in the past would have.

Even Yuki, who he'd thought he'd loved—no, that was a lie. He'd liked the thought of Yuki but had never loved her.

"Then stop bringing the topic up again."

"Daniel . . ."

"Charity . . ."

She rolled her eyes.

"Do you want a drink?" he asked, leading her over to one of the bars set up outside the banquet room.

"Seltzer water would be great."

"Seltzer water?"

"I'm working."

"Justine and Anna are providing cover. I think you can have one drink," Daniel said. He wanted this evening with Charity. Wanted to pretend that he'd have her on his arm even if she wasn't here as his bodyguard.

"Please."

She put her hand to his forehead. "Are you feeling all right?"

"Ha, ha. Are you a mixed-drink woman or a wine drinker?"

"Wine. Anything white."

"Stay here," he said, working his way through the people milling around the bar. Charity stood to one side, out of the main flow. She was vigilant and watched the crowd like the professional she was.

He saw the worry in her eyes and knew that she wasn't going to relax. Why had he dragged her here?

He knew it was to prove something to her. To prove he was a man who could give her the kind of life she deserved. And that kind of thinking was beyond stupid.

Which was the other reason why he was here with her. He needed to prove to himself that she wasn't as important as he had let her become. Wanted to do it publicly so that maybe Sekijima wouldn't go after her.

Sekijima was on his tail. The police had warned him that they'd offer what protection they could, but a threat from the Yakuza wasn't something they were exactly trained to handle. As the chief had said, most men who receive threats made by the Oyabun aren't known to the cops until they have the dead body in the morgue.

He wasn't going to end up in the morgue and he sure as hell wasn't going to let anything happen to Charity.

Someone bumped into him at the bar while he was giving the bartender his drink order. He glanced over his shoulder but the man behind him was talking to his wife, clearly not paying the least bit of attention to what was going on around him.

He bit back his own irritation, knowing it was his situation and not the man he was pissed at. He took the drinks and walked back to Charity.

"Here you go."

"Thanks. I don't like the way the light is coming in over there," she said, pointing to the plate glass windows.

"Relax or I'm going to do something outrageous."

"You're not the type," she said.

"What type am I?" he asked.

"A good man." She said it carefully, as if she knew he wasn't going to believe her.

And he didn't, but he appreciated what she said and how her eyes had softened for a moment while she gazed at him. She gave her wine to a passing waiter and took his arm. "Let's move back into the main room. We're too exposed here."

"I want to hold you in my arms."

"As long as I can see the room, I'm fine with that."

"Charity, let the job go. This night is for you."

"I can't. The job is who I am, Daniel. It always has been."

"Can you guard me on the dance floor?"

"No."

"Damn."

"Let's go home and I'll dance with you there."

But they couldn't go back home. Not yet. He needed to give Sekijima time to make his move. And since Charity and the Liberty Investigation team had shot down every possible scenario he'd come up with to make himself bait, he'd been reduced to this.

It was the best he could do on short notice and the only way he could think of to keep all three women alive. He was armed to the teeth and just praying for a glimpse of someone from the Dragon Lords.

"You're pretty tense for someone who's so busy flirting with me."

"I'm hard for you, baby—that's why I'm tense," he said, drawing her close to his side.

He wrapped his arm around her waist, pulling her into the curve of his body. The wall of windows was a problem, just as she'd mentioned. It left them too exposed. He hoped like hell this didn't turn out to be a big mistake. He drew her back, further away from the windows, and entered the ballroom as soon as the doors opened.

* * *

Something wasn't right about the way Daniel was acting. He was too flirty, too casual, and he kept them carefully in the center of the room so that everyone could see them. Normally the attention wouldn't have bothered her, but tonight, when she had the knife's edge of tension sitting heavily on her shoulders, she hated it.

He kept one hand on her waist at all times, and whenever she tried to maneuver him into a more protected position, he danced them back around so that his body was shielding hers.

"Daniel, you have to stop this."

"Stop what?"

"Trying to shield me. I want you protected by the wall and me. Stay where I put you." She had a microphone earpiece that connected her to Anna and Justine, but the girls were quiet as they performed their surveillance duties. She wished she were out there with them instead of in this crowded room with too many people to watch.

"Not a chance, Charity, unless you drew me into your arms and held me there."

She felt a little thrill at his words but pushed it aside for now. Daniel didn't talk like this normally and she knew he was up to something tonight.

"Forget it. What is with you tonight?"

"I don't know what you are talking about," he said, staring down into the cleavage revealed by her low-cut dress.

She grabbed his chin and lifted his head up so their gazes met. He hadn't ever stared at her breasts. Not even when he thought she was just . . . well, fluff.

"Ha! I think you do. You've been acting strange since we left the police station."

He refused to answer her and just kept up his vigilant watch of the room. But something was off. He didn't work the room the way Perry would have, and he didn't know very many people at the event. Why had he dragged them here?

She slipped out of his grasp and walked deliberately toward

the side of the room. She heard him curse and then start to follow her. She found the door in the back of the ballroom that lead to the service corridor where the food-and-beverage staff was all lined up and prepping to start bringing out the food.

Daniel snagged her wrist, but she kept moving down the hall until she found an isolated section. She twisted her hold on his hand, grabbed his wrist and brought it down behind his back; using her grip on him, she forced him forward against the wall and held him there.

"What are you doing? Why are we here?"

"Charity, if you like it rough—"

His words were cut off by her hand pressing against his throat. "Stop flirting with me. That's not how you normally are, and I'm not stupid or some ditzy bimbo. Why are you treating me like one?"

It was starting to hurt her feelings. She knew it shouldn't, but they'd had a connection in his condo that she'd thought went way beyond sex, yet suddenly he was treating her like some floozy he'd picked up for the night.

He jerked his hand under hers and turned so that she was pinned to the wall by his hips and hands. "I'm trying to save your life."

"What? Why? You are the one Sekijima is after."

Daniel said nothing, just kept that razor gaze of his locked on her.

"Listen, we have a plan—just let us execute it," she said. "This is what Liberty Investigations does best. Well, we really rock at everything," she continued, hoping to lighten up the mood with a little teasing, but he just continued to hold her tight in his grip.

"I can't just sit back and be the bait."

"Tell me why not. You had been planning to do just that before we even got involved."

"I'd been planning to arm myself to the teeth and lie in wait. This is different."

"How?" she said, knowing she was missing something very important that he was trying to tell her.

"I don't mind the risk to me."

She understood where he was coming from. She felt the same way about him putting his life on the line. "We're going to get Sekijima and take out the risk to you."

He shook his head. "Sekijima isn't going to allow that."

"How do you know?" she asked. He knew their enemy better than she did. And what he'd told her of him had frightened her. Not because of the danger—she could handle the situation—but the relentless way that Sekijima had pursued Daniel, the way he was systematically taking out those close to him.

"Do you think he's going to come after me?" she asked, making the only connection that made sense.

"I wish I could say no."

"What makes you think he will?

Anna, Justine, and she had been operating under the assumption that Daniel was the main target and he had let them. But they'd all have to be extra vigilant. The pattern of Sekijima's attack was finally becoming clear to her.

"He's not going to rest until he's taken down everyone near you, is he?"

"No. He's trying to destroy my house."

She knew he meant *house*, as in *life*. And she reached for him, wanting to comfort him, but he stepped away, watching her in the harsh illumination of the fluorescent lights, his green eyes hard and cold, making her shiver.

She knew there was no way that Sekijima was going to allow Daniel to live. This walk-in-the-park bodyguard assignment was turning into a very real menace. One that she might not be able to stop, the way she had with all of her other assignments.

Damn, she hated self-doubt. Of course she could keep Daniel safe. That's what she did. She was very good at her job. "Well, we're not going to let him succeed."

He shrugged.

"What?"

"Nothing. It's just a feeling I have."

"What is?"

"That we're being watched."

"When did it start?"

"At the police station."

"Dammit, I knew we should have just given our statements at the condo. Why didn't you listen to me?"

Daniel tucked a strand of hair behind her ear. "The cops weren't exactly down with your plan."

"Have you noticed anyone here tonight who looks out of place?"

"To be honest, no, but . . ."

"Your gut is telling you something's wrong. Fine, then let's figure it out. That doesn't tell me why you are treating me like some kind of high-class escort."

"I . . . this is not part of my plan," he said, kissing her fiercely and stepping back. "I want Sekijima's people to think you are alone. I can't take a chance that he might suspect how much you mean to me."

Daniel had said more than he'd meant to, but having the words out there made it easier. "Now, stay where I put you and keep acting like you don't have a brain."

"Why?"

"Because I could never be really attracted to someone who was stupid."

"Me, either," she said.

Daniel fought the knowledge that she was the perfect woman for him. He knew he wasn't meant for forever; he'd only known Charity for a day but there was something about her that drew him.

He knew himself well enough to know that he wasn't walking away from this relationship with her unscathed. And for the first time he had something he didn't want to lose. He knew that keeping Charity was out of the question.

No matter how she looked at him now, once the job was over she'd realize that she deserved better. He was still more street thug than civilized, and if he'd learned anything throughout the course of his life, he knew that he would never be able to outrun the boy who'd grown up on the streets.

"Why are you watching me like that?" she asked. He heard the note of concern in her voice.

No one had ever worried over him the way she did. One part of him, the very cynical part that had been betrayed by the only person he'd ever allowed himself to depend on, cautioned that he was paying her to care. She had to protect him because that was her job.

But he'd always been a good judge of people and he could see the depth of the caring in her eyes. She wasn't watching him because it was her job anymore. Now she was watching him because she wanted to keep him safe.

He wanted to hug her close, wrap his arms around her and pick her up and carry her out of this place. Take her and hide away with her where Sekimjima would never find her.

But he couldn't.

He kissed her again. Slowly and lingeringly, because he hated knowing he was going to have to treat her like she was nothing to him. And that was going to be harder than he'd thought it would be.

"I want you to stay where I put you when we go back in there."

"That's not happening. What did you have in mind?"

"I'm going to case the room and see if I can find the person working for Sekijima."

"Will you know them on sight?"

"No, but I will know who he's sent by the way they move."

"I can help."

He leaned over and kissed her. She sounded confident and

just a little bloodthirsty. He loved that about her. "Help me by sitting at the table and looking like you are interested in me for my money."

Charity narrowed her eyes and crossed her arms over her ample breasts. "I hate that. I'm supposed to be guarding you."

"You will be. I'll stay in sight the entire time. And you'll be a nice distraction for anyone who's watching the room."

"A distraction?" she said.

"Don't tell me you haven't used your looks as a weapon before."

She shrugged, tipped her head to the side, and gave him a really flirty look. She licked her full lips and subtly shifted her shoulders, somehow making her breasts seem more prominent. She opened her mouth and he was enthralled.

"Like this?"

"Hell, yes."

She shook her head. "I hate doing it."

"You did it the first moment we met."

She wasn't surprised that he'd called her on it. She knew that most men didn't realize what she was doing, but Daniel caught on quicker than most.

"Okay. I'll do it but you have to take Justine with you. You can't go out like that without backup. And if I'm putting on a show, I won't be able to get to you quickly."

Daniel struggled not to grimace. Justine didn't like him and had made no bones about it. "Fine."

He stood behind Charity, breathing in the scent of her, hoping he'd always be able to recall it, while she contacted Justine. A few minutes later the other woman appeared.

Tall, though not as tall as Charity, Justine was a brunette, and dressed up didn't look nearly as tough as she did in her normal jeans and leather jacket.

"You're staring," she said, all tough-nosed attitude.

"You look like a woman."

Charity laughed but Justine just gave him an aggrieved look. "Enough with the small talk—let's go."

Daniel walked away without looking back at Charity, something he'd always been able to do, but this time he was aware of her there, waiting.

And he knew that no matter how much he tried to pretend otherwise, she was important to him.

Chapter Seventeen

Doubt is not a pleasant condition, but certainty is absurd.

—Voltaire

Walking through the shadows, Daniel felt the absurdity of what he was doing. Skulking in darkness wasn't the way to draw Sekijima out, and he knew it, but as Voltaire had said, doubt was a much more realistic way of dealing with life. And he doubted very much that Sekijima was ready to end the game.

Finding his minions was the only thing that Daniel could do, and he was damned tired of being a pawn.

"What are we looking for?" Justine asked.

Daniel spared a glance for the woman following behind him. "I'm guessing a single hit man. It doesn't have to be a man. They'll be very hard to spot because they are trained to blend in. My money's on someone of Japanese descent because Sekijima doesn't trust Americans."

"Why doesn't he?"

"Because he was once betrayed by one."

"You?"

Daniel shrugged. "Have you ever seen a sniper before?"

"Golly, gee, no. This is my first day on the job."

"Does being a smart-ass make you feel better?" he asked, unable to help himself.

"Yes, it does. Especially when I'm around arrogant men who refuse to listen."

Daniel didn't rise to the bait. Instead he sank back into the shadows of the room. He could see Charity from where he stood. She was a golden goddess. Everyone around her leaned in, listening to what she was saying, the men enthralled by her beauty, the woman enticed by the openness of her smile.

Suddenly he was very certain of one thing. It was like a moment of clarity in a world he no longer was sure of: he knew that Charity was the one woman he'd never forget.

He could only hope that Sekijima hadn't been watching him too carefully or his old friend was going to know that Charity was way more than arm candy.

"Stop staring and get to work."

"I'm not staring. I'm scanning the room. What do you think of the woman at the table to the left of the podium in the second row?"

"She's talking to her tablemates but . . . there is something in her eyes. She's watching the room when she thinks no one is looking."

"Yes," Daniel said. "Can Anna run a check on her?"

"Yeah, one second," Justine said. She spoke into her wireless microphone and then brought up her BlackBerry, taking a quick photo of the woman. "Anna will run a check on her photo."

"How long until we know?"

"Five minutes, maybe longer. I've got my eye on her. Keep casing the room."

Daniel did, leaving Justine behind and searching all the people there. He tried to let go of the man he'd become and get back to the Yakuza he'd once been. He needed those instincts that had been honed in blood and betrayal.

He stopped keeping an eye on Charity because he trusted her to take care of herself. And he couldn't really sink into the past and those instincts he needed while he looked at her.

The years and the layers fell away and he moved more easily in the darkened shadows at the edge of the ballroom. The sounds even became sharper and he could hear the minute changes in conversations. The whispered confessions of two women at a table in front of him. The booming cadence of the oil baron from Texas. And the German accent of the art dealers sitting at the corner table.

Finally he heard the sound he was waiting for. The choppy, long vowels of Japanese, the rhythm and lilt in the speech pattern that couldn't be hidden in colloquial American.

He moved closer to the sounds, stopping when he realized it was an elderly couple. He doubted Sekijima would send an elderly couple to kill him, but he remembered what Voltaire said. Doubt wasn't absurd, certainty was.

He moved up behind him and the man turned as he approached. Daniel knew his instincts were right. The man had Yakuza connections, but he wasn't the hit man sent to take him out tonight.

The man tensed as he glanced down at Daniel's right hand and saw the missing fingertip. He saw the fear in the older man's eyes and realized that he might not be the only target in the room tonight.

That would play perfectly into Sekijima's plans. Kill this man in retaliation and leave Daniel thinking he might be the target. A part of him wanted to introduce himself and then somehow try to get the couple to safety but he couldn't.

If he did, he might jeopardize Charity and her team. And for once he was loyal to a woman. Was that right? How the hell had that happened?

He didn't know, just kept moving past the table where the Japanese couple sat. He hoped the older man was savvy enough to protect himself and his woman. But that wasn't Daniel's concern.

He kept moving until he realized that he'd checked out all of the tables and the hit man wasn't at any of them. He knew a second before he felt the touch of a feminine hand against his neck that he'd made a mistake.

"Come with me, Mr. Williams, or the woman dies."

He glanced over his shoulder, knowing he could shoot her before she had a chance to stop him, but that if he made a move to harm Sekijima's messenger, Charity would die. A quick glance to the table where he'd left her confirmed that she was no longer there.

Inane conversation was exhausting, and Charity was tense. She tried to keep up the pretense of liking being the center of attention but after twenty minutes of watching Daniel and Justine case the room she couldn't sit still any longer.

"I need a drink," she said.

"I'll get you one," Wolfgang offered. Considering he'd been staring at her chest all evening, she wasn't surprised.

"That's okay. I need to stretch my legs."

She left the table and made her way through the crowd.

"Charity Keone?"

"Yes?"

"Hi, I'm Amanda Markell. We were models together back in Paris."

The Eurasian woman was simply beautiful but Charity couldn't recall having met her before, and usually she had a photographic memory for faces. She was running through those early modeling days in her mind. Amanda leaned forward to embrace her and Charity did the same.

"Don't," Anna said in her ear.

That minute warning from Anna wasn't enough, as she felt the sharp point of a knife in her side. The woman wielding the knife wrapped her arm around Charity's shoulders.

"Smile and excuse yourself if you want to live."

Charity smiled at the woman and started to grab her wrist to change their positions so she'd have power. "Not so fast or Daniel dies. You don't want to lose your client, do you?"

"I haven't lost one yet."

"Then you're due, aren't you?"

"Due? It's going to take more than a knife to take Mr. Williams out of the game."

"Move toward the back of the room," Amanda said.

Charity ran through all her options as she moved slowly toward the back. She was wearing a pair of specially made stilettos with blades embedded into them. Her dress, however, didn't have a slit to the thigh. Only to the knee, and that would hamper her getting off a good roundhouse kick.

And her hair was hanging loose around her shoulders. Damn vanity. She'd worn it down because Daniel had asked her to before they'd left. A ponytail would be more practical in a fight. With her hair loose, there was a very good chance it could be used against her.

The pressure of the knife against her side never let up. She could feel it cutting into her skin through the thin fabric of her dress. She also felt the warmth of her own blood as it started to drip from the wound.

As soon as they stepped out of the room, Charity grabbed the wrist holding the knife to her ribs and jerked out of Amanda's grasp. She squeezed Amanda's wrist, slamming her hand against the brick wall until it opened and the knife fell to the ground with a clatter.

Charity kicked it out of Amanda's reach and spun away to grab the weapon. She was drawn up short when Amanda grasped Charity's hair and yanked back hard. Tears burned in Charity's eyes but she ignored the pain. Her gun was in a thigh holster so she wouldn't ruin the line of her dress.

What a stupid place for the gun, she thought. She spun on her heel to face Amanda, then balled up her fist and hit Amanda in the jaw. The other woman's head snapped back, but she didn't let go of Charity's hair. Instead she twisted the strands around her fist, drawing Charity even closer to her.

Dammit. She hit Amanda again, holding her body loose and

torquing her hips to keep her rhythm. Her head ached with each move but she felt the other woman weakening.

"I'm on my way," Anna said. "Justine's on Daniel."

"I've got this."

"Bloody hell," Anna said. "I don't—"

"Go, Anna. I'm not in over my head," Charity said.

But Amanda yanked hard on her hair. "I think you are."

She flicked the earpiece out of Charity's ear and onto the floor. "I don't think you need that."

Charity wasn't interested in talking to Amanda. She wanted to get free and turn the tables. She had to concentrate. She grabbed Amanda's free hand and pulled the arm over her own left shoulder and toward her waist, then bent and flipped Amanda onto the floor.

Amanda didn't let go of Charity's hair and she felt a few strands ripping out by their roots. Charity grunted in pain and brought the sharp edge of her stiletto down on Amanda's arm, pinning her to the floor.

Amanda drew her nails down Charity's leg, digging deep until blood welled from the scratches. Charity drew back and hit the woman again.

She hated this kind of fight. She wanted to get Amanda up off the floor and subdue her. Amanda kicked hard at the back of Charity's knee, knocking her off balance for a second.

Charity dropped to the floor next to her. She grabbed Amanda's arm and twisted it hard behind her, forcing the other woman to roll over, and then Charity drew her to her feet. She had flex cuffs in her purse which she'd stupidly left at the table, so she had nothing with which to bind the other woman's wrists. So she found the carotid artery and applied pressure until she felt Amanda go limp and lowered her to the ground. She picked up the knife and the earpiece.

"I need cuffs. My attacker is subdued."

"On my way," Anna said. "Daniel just got into a black Mercedes without plates."

"Is Justine following?"

"Yes, but I think we're going to be needed," Anna said. She stepped into the hallway a second later.

Charity cuffed Amanda and between her and Anna they were able to heft her down the hall and out of the hotel.

"I'll take her back to our headquarters and question her," Anna said. "Once I have her secured I can join up with you and Justine."

"Sounds good. Find out where they are taking Daniel if you can."

"Justine won't lose them."

"I know, but we can call for backup if we know where we are going."

Anna nodded. Charity pulled a duffel bag from the trunk of the car and changed out of the evening gown into her leather pants, T-shirt, and jacket. She moved her gun from the thigh holster to her shoulder, added another Sig Sauer at the small of her back, and pulled her hair up into a ponytail.

No more doing things to please Daniel—she'd almost gotten them both killed. Which was a lesson she'd thought she'd learned a long time ago.

Daniel knew that anyone who took Charity was getting more than they bargained for. But he did feel a clench of fear deep in his stomach at the thought of her somehow falling into Sekijima's hands.

He went quietly with the woman who held the gun steady in the small of his back. He knew that the Liberty Investigations team was watching him and the hotel and felt fairly certain they'd put a tail on him and his captor. But the last thing he wanted to do was lead them into a trap.

He was led to a black Mercedes. "Get inside."

"Thanks, but I have my own ride."

The woman tightened her grip on his arm. "Don't make this harder on yourself."

Daniel knew he could take the woman. He jerked to the side to lead her off balance, then hit her with a quick upper jab to the sternum. Her breath rushed out of her lungs and she fell back on the ground. He brought his foot down hard on her wrist and bent to take the gun.

As soon as he stood up, he was hit from behind by a man. His own wrist was grabbed and he was jerked around, his hands brought together behind his back and cuffed.

The man who'd hit him offered his hand to the girl. She wobbled a little as he helped her to her feet.

The man punched him in the gut twice and then hit him in the face, snapping his head back. Daniel tasted blood on his lip. He licked at the blood as the man drew back to hit him again. He went with the punch, stepping back, then delivered a vertical kick to his opponent's throat, trying to crush his esophagus, but the man fell backward and then rolled to his feet.

He hit Daniel again with a kick aimed for the groin. Daniel turned and deflected the kick but took a hard hit in the thigh. He stumbled backward for a second, then kicked the man again with a solid roundhouse to the other man's jaw. He stumbled backward and Daniel kept coming, hitting him with a front snap kick and then another roundhouse kick, this time to the solar plexus. The man doubled over, and as he started to stand, Daniel straightened his spine and ran forward, head-butting him.

He used the high section of his forehead to deliver the blow to his opponent's nose. Blood splurted from his face and Daniel stayed where he was, hitting the man one more time. He heard the man groan as he stumbled toward the ground. Dammit, he'd hoped the blow would knock his opponent unconscious—instead, he seemed to have just bloodied his nose. Daniel rammed him hard with his shoulder and the man bit down on Daniel's arm. Daniel jerked free, his entire body in pain.

"Enough," Sekijima said from the car. "Gumi, you drive. Suki, escort Mr. Williams to the car."

Suki reached for his bound arms, pulling him toward the car with more strength than he'd suspected she had. He jerked off balance.

The barrel of a Sig Sauer semiautomatic handgun emerged from the car. A bullet hit him in the thigh and he moaned, struggling to stay on his feet and not react to the pain.

"Daniel, get in the car or I'll kill you and your girl right now."

"Isn't that the plan?" he asked, refusing to give in to the fear that the thought of Charity in Sekijima's hands evoked.

"Indeed, but not in this alleyway."

Gumi got up from the ground and shoved Daniel into the backseat of the car. Suki got into front seat on the passenger side. Gumi got behind the wheel and started the car.

Daniel sank back into the leather seats, working his wrists to try to free them, but the cuffs were too tight. He deliberately tugged harder until he felt the cuffs cut into the skin of his wrist, knowing the blood would make his hands slippery and give him a chance to slip free.

His ribs ached and his face was pulsing in time to his heartbeat. And deep inside he ached for Charity, for the risks he'd taken a lifetime ago that she was now paying for.

He glanced over at the man sitting next to him. They had the same missing right digit. They had the same tattooed dragon on their backs and they had the same hatred in their hearts. Only a man who was once closer than a brother could understand betrayal the way Daniel and Sekijima did.

His enemy—a man he'd once left for dead—sat less than three feet away from him. He ignored Sekijima, stalling for time as he marshaled his thoughts. He needed to know if his enemy wanted something more than he wanted him dead.

"How'd you do it?" Daniel asked.

"How'd I do what?" Sekijima asked, his Japanese accent still thick after all these years.

"Come back from the dead," Daniel specified. Killing was something he knew inside and out. Usually when he made a hit, his target wasn't a threat again.

"You aren't as good as you once were, Gashira Hosa," Sekijima said, watching him with those shrewd black eyes of his.

Daniel felt the failure deep inside himself. A part of him demanded payment from himself for the mistake, and he knew that before the night was through he'd be in the position to kill Sekijima again—and this time he was going to make damned sure the man stayed dead.

"I'm not your second anymore."

Sekijima lifted his hand and rubbed the thin scar around his neck where Daniel had cut him with a wire. The neck injury had been up close and personal, the way Daniel had wanted it. He should have bled out, Daniel thought.

"I'm well aware of that, but you do still owe the Dragon Lords." The fact that Sekijima was back with the Dragon Lords was significant. He would have had to overthrow the Oyabun who'd taken his place—his own brother.

It was another chink between them. The man he'd known and admired had put family at the front of all of his actions. And if Sekijima had killed his brother . . .

Daniel shook his head. "That debt was paid a long time ago."

Sekijima took a small, thin cigarillo from a case and lit it. The smell was pungent and familiar, taking Daniel back to his childhood.

"I'll decide when it's paid."

So that's what this was all about. The roughing-up of his staff was retaliation for leaving his old friend dead. Sekijima wanted him for something else—he knew what it was. The old business scheme. The importation of people and not products. Smuggling.

Could he do it again? Hell, yes, if it meant that Charity would walk free and live out the rest of her days happily, then he'd gladly sell his soul to Sekijima. Daniel didn't fool himself that if he got back into bed with Sekijima, he'd be able to save any of the goodness he'd found in the last few years. The blackness in his heart would grow and eclipse him.

"What do you want?" he said levelly, looking at a man who'd once had a shred of decency in him that had been bred out over the years.

"The same thing you do."

"And that is?" Daniel asked, trying not to feel like he was looking into a mirror.

"For the girl to live."

"What girl?"

"Your girl. The tall blonde. We found evidence on the plane that you used her body," Sekijima said.

"She means nothing to me," Daniel said. He wasn't ready to play into Sekijima's hands just yet. He had to be careful how and if he played his trump card. Giving up his soul was something he'd promised himself he'd never do, but to save his heart, to save Charity, it was the very least he could do.

Daniel fought not to react. He didn't want anyone to know what had happened privately between him and Charity.

And he had no doubt that Charity *was* his heart. Just the thought of her in trouble or captured made him want to do whatever it took to keep her safe.

"For your sake, I hope so."

Chapter Eighteen

You just can't beat the person who never gives up.
—George "Babe" Ruth

Charity tried to keep the Babe's motto in the front of her mind as she drove through the Seattle traffic. She wasn't a big baseball fan, but come on, everyone loved the Babe.

In her mind was the fact that Sekijima hadn't given up. And Daniel never would. There was no way for anything to end between the two men that didn't involve bloodshed.

"Where are you, Justine?"

"Following the Mercedes. It's turned into a warehouse area. I'm sending you the GPS coordinates. I'm going to have to drop back or I'll be spotted."

Charity received the GPS coordinates in her BlackBerry. The navigational system automatically spit out three different courses she could take. She chose the most direct. "I'm en route."

"Where's Anna?"

"She took Amanda to lockup," Charity said.

"Amanda?"

"That's the woman who tried to use me as bait," Charity said, trying to find the calm center she'd need to function efficiently, but it was damned hard. She'd lost her client. She never lost a person she was guarding before, and that was because Daniel had insisted on acting on his own.

Hell, she was smarter than that. She should have put her foot down instead of caving like she had.

"Ah. Is she still breathing?" Justine asked.

Charity shook her head. As much as she'd wanted to choke the life out of that bitch who tried to use her, she hadn't. She wasn't in the vigilante business anymore.

"Yes. I'm a bodyguard, not a hit man."

"True enough. Eurasian super-model?"

"Yes, that's her."

"She was eyeing your man," Justine said.

"He's not my man. He's our client."

"You're not still telling yourself that?" Justine asked.

"Justine, focus on the job."

"I can do two things at once. Men love that."

"What's with you?"

"Giddy, ready to fight. It feels like months since I've seen any action."

Charity's entire body ached. She hated getting hit. Justine liked a good fistfight, said the blows made her feel alive, but she wasn't like that. She preferred the distance of a hand gun. Didn't really like the personal feel of hand to hand combat.

With a weapon she could distance herself, and she needed that distance to keep her cool and enable her to do her job. She still did it with hand to hand, but she could remember the feel of the other person under her hands.

"It's only been a little over a week since your bruises faded from your last assignment," Charity pointed out. She worried about Justine. Her friend was getting more tightly wound and needed to go out and fight more often.

"I'm fine. It's you I'm worried about. You okay?"

"Yeah," Charity said, though she doubted that she was anymore. How could her entire life change in one day? The answer was simple—it hadn't. She'd been changing for a while now. It was only Daniel who was making her realize what she'd been hiding from. "Are you on foot?"

"Will be in a second. I'm arming up."

"Arming up? How many are in there with him?"

"There were three in the car when they took him. I don't know how many we'll find when we go in."

"I'm armed, so we should be good."

"Should I take the RPG launcher?"

"Not unless you're planning to burn down the entire ware-house area."

"You have a point," Justine said. "They beat him up, Char-ity. This isn't just blackmail or extortion. They want his blood."

Charity's gut tightened and she found that cold rage that she'd used to kill her parents' murderer years ago. She'd al-ways been aware of it there in the bottom of her soul, but she kept her distance from that part of herself.

"Is he okay?"

"Yeah, he gave as good as he got," Justine said, and there was a note of respect in her voice that had never been there before.

"He always does."

"You'd know." She heard the solid thunk of the trunk clos-ing and then nothing but wind. Justine was on the move.

"It's not like that," Charity said, but it *was* like that.

"Yeah, it is—you're just afraid to admit it. He's not someone you can manipulate, like Senator Perry."

"You're right—he's nothing like Perry."

Charity made a turn that took her down toward the ware-houses, wanting to focus on rescuing Daniel and taking care of the threat to him. And then what? She had no idea.

"I'm going to park a few blocks over."

"Good. I'm tracking him. He's not in the first two ware-houses on the left—closest to the water."

"Affirmative. I'm on my way. I'll start on the right and work my way to you."

"Sounds good. I'm going silent."

"Affirmative," Charity said.

She ran quickly through the streets, loosening her body up. Her muscles still ached but the adrenaline pumping through her body dulled the pain. Her ponytail hit the back of her neck as she ran.

She tried not to think about everything Justine had said. Tried not to imagine Daniel beat up and in pain. She wanted . . . something she wasn't going to find with him.

He gave as good as he got.

Those words echoed in her mind, reminding her that he wasn't like the other CEOs she'd guarded. He was a man who knew how to hold his own with the dregs of society. He was a street punk who'd made good but she knew he hadn't lost that part of himself.

She didn't mind that because it made him who he was. But she also knew that there was no future with a street punk.

The Mercedes pulled right up to one of the biggest warehouses that Williams Import/Export owned. Daniel felt like a complete idiot for not expecting Sekijima to hit here. The only excuse he had was that all of the other attacks had been personal.

"Get out," Sekijima said as Gumi opened the door.

"Make me," Daniel said, having decided he wasn't going down easy. His thigh was aching and he felt his pulse as the blood slowly oozed from the gunshot wound. His wrists were one big ache. Yet he wasn't going to cooperate.

"Daniel, I only need you alive, not in one piece," Sekijima said, pulling his gun from the shoulder holster.

"Why do you need me?" Daniel asked. It was the one thing he hadn't been able to figure out. Sekijima's revenge he understood.

"I want this business back."

"It's not yours."

"I'm not going to argue with you on this. You will take on a new partner—Gumi."

"Yes, sir?"

"Is our friend inside?"

"Yes, sir."

"Daniel, let's go. You can either walk in there on your own . . ."

He hated threats. "Like I'm afraid of you."

"You always had more balls than brains."

"And I always knew how to use both."

"True enough," Sekijima said, lowering the barrel of the gun toward his uninjured leg. Daniel swung toward the open door, stepping out on that uninjured leg. He needed at least one leg that was fully functional if he was going to save himself and Charity.

Daniel ached from head to toe as he walked into the building. His night shift security guard was slumped at an odd angle just inside the doorway. And not bound. Daniel knew the man was dead. The lights in the office at the back of the warehouse were on and his night shift supervisor was visible.

Corbin's face was bloodied and he had that dazed look that came from being hit too many times. He perked up when he saw Daniel but resignation spread over the other man's face quickly as he realized that Sekijima held a gun at Daniel's back.

There were two underlings working Corbin over. They had his hands bound above his head to a rope that was suspended over the exposed iron rafter in the ceiling. There were no ceiling panels in this office.

"What do you want from him?" Daniel asked.

"Nothing. He's your man, so he's our enemy."

"Let him go."

"Ah, Daniel, has it really been so long? We let no one go."

Corbin blanched, his knees buckling as the impact of Sekijima's words sank in. He noticed the long cuts on Corbin's arms. They'd stripped the shirt from the other man so Daniel could see the mottled bruising along his ribs and stomach.

Daniel shook his head. "This man has nothing to do with the business between us. I'll consider his release a goodwill gesture."

"I don't want your goodwill."

Fucking bastard, Daniel thought. He tested the strength of his injured thigh, leaning heavily on it and waiting to see if it would take his weight.

He'd be able to lash out with it but he needed room. And this office was small and crowded with six people in it. And Corbin, strung up as he was.

"You do if you want your new partner to survive. You can't watch me 24/7 and I'm not going to cooperate unless you stop killing my people."

Sekijima shook his head. "I'll consider it. For now that man stays where he is."

Suki returned to the room and walked over to Sekijima. She put her hand on his shoulder and then slid it down his chest, leaning in low to whisper in his ear. She let her breasts brush against Sekijima's arm. Daniel knew that the woman was Sekijima's lover.

Sekijima nodded at whatever she said and then turned to Gumi. "Tie him up and then meet me in the other warehouse."

"Are we done?"

"Not by a long shot, Daniel. We just have a loose end to wrap up."

Charity, he wondered? He wanted to know she was safe but knew she could handle herself. He was going to have to trust that she was everything she'd said she was. Of course, he'd seen the proof firsthand.

Gumi would be easy to take. Daniel shifted to the side so he could assess the other man better. Sekijima returned, raising his left hand and clubbing him on the side of the head with the gun in his fist.

He blacked out as he fell to the floor. The blackout was momentary and he struggled not to give in to the darkness. He lay still on the floor.

"Get him up and in that chair."

Daniel was lifted and placed in a chair. His bound hands burned as Gumi released the flex cuffs and tied his arms to the arms of the chair. His feet were then bound to the legs of the chair. He kept his head down, trying to act as if he were still woozy from the hit.

Sekijima grabbed his chin and wrenched his head higher. Staring into the black eyes of the man he'd once called brother really brought home to Daniel how much his life had changed.

"What's going on?" Charity asked as she joined Justine on the roof of the most central warehouse.

"They just took Daniel in there," Justine said, pointing to the door immediately to their left. "Where is the security team that works for Williams Import?"

"I have no idea. Alonzo's out of commission, so it could be that whoever the second in command is . . . isn't that competent."

"Could be?"

"Sarcasm isn't really helpful right now."

"To each his own."

"Stop it, Justine."

"Sorry. I'm edgy. One guy is already dead in there."

"Daniel?"

"No, an older man. Near the doorway," Justine said, handing Charity her high-powered binoculars.

She adjusted the night vision goggles and saw the man Justine had described. "Where's Daniel?"

"They walked toward the rear of the building and I lost them."

"What about the listening device we had on Daniel?"

"Anna's monitoring that one."

"Anna? You there?"

"Yes. Just back—sorry. I had to let the machine record Daniel's piece. We need one more girl to really function well in this kind of situation."

"Tell Sam," Justine said.

"I plan to. Okay, there was the sound of a fight," Anna said. "Two people named Gumi and Suki. I'm running the names but they are common in Japan and I doubt I'll find a match."

"I witnessed the fight. I can give you a description if they get away tonight," Justine said.

"Good. Sam wants everyone in custody and said to keep the body count low."

"We've already got one."

"Ours?"

"Theirs."

"Bloody hell, I don't like this setup. Sekijima wants Daniel to take on a silent partner. He is using Charity as bait. He must not know that you escaped."

"Are you sure?"

"Well, he could be bluffing."

"Yeah, well, Daniel probably doesn't know what to believe," Charity said.

Justine shook her head. "He's in there because he believes they have you and he wants to rescue you."

Charity didn't want to believe that. If that was true, then she'd just compromised his safety by being intimate with him.

"How are we getting him out of there?" Charity asked, focusing on the one thing she could do right now, and that was her job.

"I say we both go in, and go in hard. Weapons drawn, bullets flying. Take out as many of the bastards as we can," Justine said.

"Did you hear what I said about body count? Sam wants it low," Anna said through their earpieces.

Charity sat up so she was watching the rooftop and their back trail while Justine kept her eye on the warehouse.

"I'm just saying it's quick and efficient and I haven't heard any other ideas."

Charity ran the different variables through her head. Daniel would operate under the assumption that she was captured. He would assume she'd try to escape and he would . . . what? Would he wait until he knew she was safe before he made a move?

"We need to let Daniel know that I'm not captured," Charity said. "Then he can focus on himself and stop trying to protect me."

In the background she heard the sound of Anna's fingers moving over her keyboard. "I can send an alert to his Black-Berry, but all that will do is vibrate it. Can he read his messages?"

"Ah, no. He's tied up," Justine said.

"So we're stuck with him not knowing," Charity said. She couldn't give a definite reason, but she was sure it was imperative that Daniel know she was safe. Otherwise, she feared he'd end up dying in there to protect her.

"Give me a minute," Anna said in that distracted way she had when she was working on a problem.

"Then my plan is the best one. That way we can hit Seki-jima hard, eliminate at least part of his crew, and then rescue Daniel," Justine insisted.

"What if he just kills Daniel while we're blowing the hell out of his crew?"

Justine was silent. Charity kept vigilant, knowing Justine would have picked a secure location for the lookout, but always knowing better than to let her guard down.

"Okay, I can send a message via the security system. It won't be much. I wonder if he knows Morse code?"

"Anna."

"It was just a thought. Hold on. There are three computers on in the building . . ."

"No," Charity said. "You can't send a message—we have no idea who'd read it."

"Well, I'm fresh out of ideas then," Anna said.

"I'll go in and get him out. Justine will provide cover and backup. Anna, are you on your way here?"

"Yes, I am. But still about ten minutes out."

"Should we wait?"

"Yes," Justine said. "I want to go in."

Charity knew that Justine was a logical choice to go in with her to rescue Daniel. But she didn't want to wait.

"How about you wait for Anna and I'll get a closer look? See exactly what we're up against."

"How about no?" Justine said.

"I'm going. It makes sense. Every second we stay here could be the difference between life and death—his."

"Dammit."

"Bloody hell, you two fight too much. Go ahead, Charity, but don't move in unless we're both in position."

"Affirmative," Charity said. She knew that she'd move if she thought Daniel's life was in danger. She wasn't about to lose him.

Chapter Nineteen

Self-reverence, self-knowledge, self-control. These
three alone lead life to sovereign power.
                                    —Alfred, Lord Tennyson

Daniel wished that real life was a little more like the movies. Then he'd have a lucky lighter or a knife up his sleeve. But instead he was tied to a chair, and short of falling over and trying to roll out of the room, he had few options.

"Corbin?" Daniel asked as soon as they were alone. The other man was suspended on the tips of his toes, head forward.

"Yes?" Corbin didn't lift his head, just continued to stare at the floor.

"You okay?"

"I've been better," Corbin said. "What the hell is going on?"

"I'm being blackmailed."

"I hate to break this to you, but this is more than blackmail."

"True, that. I'm not planning to let it go any further."

"Great intentions, but we're both kind of stuck here," Corbin said.

"Can you get free?" Daniel had to ask. He knew that with Sekijima watching, Gumi had bound him very tightly to the chair.

"I'll try."

"You haven't?"

"Uh, no," Corbin said a little sheepishly. He lifted his feet and let his arms take the weight of his body. The knots simply tightened and didn't give way. Not that Daniel had expected them to. Sekijima hadn't become Oyabun by being incompetent.

"We're going to die here," Corbin said.

The other man's voice was shaky, and Daniel had no real way to reassure him. That wasn't something he'd ever been good at—comforting anyone. And somehow he didn't think he ever would be.

"Not if I can help it."

He visually searched the room, looking for something they could use to cut themselves free. If he could get closer to the metal filing cabinet he might be able to use the edge to cut the rope.

But they'd bound his legs so that his knees were bent and only the tips of his toes rested on the ground. He tried shifting in his chair but it wouldn't budge. And he could tell from the way that Corbin looked that the other man was close to losing it, to just saying to hell with everything.

He spotted a packing tape dispenser with a razor edge attached on top of the cabinet. If he'd been bound like Corbin, he'd be able to swing his legs and . . .

"Can you kick out far enough to reach the filing cabinet?"

"I'm not sure, why?"

"See that roll of packing tape?"

"What are we going to use it for? We're already bound."

"We need the blade."

"How is that going to work?"

"The edge is serrated."

"I get that part. But how are we going to use it . . ."

"Kick it over to me. I just need to be able to get my finger on it. Umm . . . try to aim for my left side."

"I'll try, Daniel. I'm not sure I can do it."

Daniel saw the doubt and fear in Corbin's eyes. "This isn't our last hope. Take your time. I know you can do it."

Corbin swung his legs and missed the cabinet completely. The other man groaned as his arms took the weight of his swinging body. Daniel needed Corbin's help, but he wasn't sure the other man was up to the task.

"Sorry."

Daniel shook his head. He couldn't be demanding or harsh with Corbin. He had to be the man he'd learned to be in the corporate world. "It's okay. You're doing great. Take a deep breath this time. Can you use one foot for balance?"

"Let me try it."

He did and it worked a lot better. Corbin's leg reached the edge of the metal vertical file, but not quite the top of it.

"Extend your lower leg a little further. You're going to need more momentum . . ."

With a burst of energy, Corbin lifted his foot and skimmed the top of the filing cabinet, catching papers as well as the packing tape dispenser, which flew from the cabinet and landed on the edge of Daniel's knee.

Daniel rocked backward quickly, keeping the tape in his lap. He extended his fingers, catching the edge of the tape and drawing it closer. He worked the dispenser with his finger until he got the serrated edge where wanted it.

"Hurry," Corbin said.

Daniel tuned the other man out. He knew that only patience would free him from the chair. He rocked the blade back and forth in his fingers, feeling it cut into the bottom of his palm but watching as it slowly penetrated the nylon rope, the threads slowly coming undone. He didn't have to cut it all the way through—he just needed enough give to move his hand.

"Daniel—"

"Be quiet, Corbin. Conserve your strength. I'm going to be free in a few minutes and then you will be and we're getting out of here."

Corbin nodded. "I thought I saw a shadow reflected in the plate glass windows."

"Where?"

"Deep in the left corner."

Daniel continued working the blade but kept his eyes on that corner. He didn't see anything at first but then noticed a pool of black stillness in the darkness. He knew that someone was there, watching. Sensed it was Bo Long, his old rival. He wanted to believe it was the team from Liberty Investigations but suspected it was one of Sekijima's men instead.

A flash of movement told him that there was some type of confrontation going on over there. And that distraction was exactly what he needed to get out of here.

Charity was in position when she heard Sekijima leave the building. Using the night vision goggles, she could see Daniel under the bare light of an exposed bulb in the office. He looked a little worse for wear, but determined.

Daniel was cutting the hell out of his wrist. She couldn't go down because it'd be stupid to risk her life when she'd have backup in less then ten minutes. But dammit, she wanted to.

She was tense, and the focus she felt in herself she'd only felt one other time . . . when she'd gone after Kenkichi. She'd carefully buried that part of herself, made sure she could keep that killing rage bottled up. But seeing Daniel bound, his employee helpless and beaten . . . it brought everything to the surface.

"I'm going in," she said.

"Wait—we're almost in position."

"I can't."

She had opened an air vent in the side of the warehouse and now lowered herself onto one of the steel beams that ran along the ceiling of the building. She had to bend low but was careful to keep her center of gravity so she didn't lose her balance.

She moved the way she'd been taught to by her Master in

Kobe. Quickly, silently, deadly. She reached for the knife that she'd always worn back then but the holster wasn't on her chest. She only had her gun, a weapon that was noisy but effective.

She felt someone behind her and glanced back to see Justine on her heels. "We're going to talk later."

"Whatever. We have to get Daniel and the other man free before Sekijima gets to them."

"I'll lower you. You can cut them free. Anna's providing cover from the roof, and I've got your back from here."

Charity nodded. She already had the harness on, having put it on back at the hotel. She knew that Justine and Anna would have one on as well—they were always ready for any possibility.

Justine looped a heavy climbing rope around the steel bar and secured it, then let it drop down. Daniel glanced up at them and stopped sawing at the rope at his wrist. He shook his head.

She tipped her head to the side, trying to figure out what he was saying. He arched one eyebrow at her and nodded to the corner of the warehouse.

"I think someone is over there," she said to Justine, careful to keep her voice almost soundless. Dropping the rope had given away her position, but anyone watching wouldn't be able to ascertain if there was only one person or more. "It a good bet he knows I'm here."

"But I'm a variable."

"Yup. You want to go do a little hunting."

Justine smiled before disappearing. Charity clipped her harness to the rope and slowly lowered herself. She had to maneuver her body through the cage where the ceiling tiles should have been, but in less than a minute she was on the floor near Daniel.

She unclipped her harness; bending low, she took the knife from her ankle sheath and cut him free. "I need a weapon," he said.

She handed him her spare semiautomatic from the holster at the small of her back. Up close she saw the bruising on his face and the wound on his thigh oozing blood. She wanted to wrap her arms around him and hug him close, then stash him someplace safe while she found Sekijima.

"Why are you staring at me?" he asked.

"You look a lot worse than you did earlier . . ."

"So do you."

She shook her head. "This is about you."

"It's about us now. Sekijima isn't going to let either of us walk away unless I give him what he wants."

"Daniel—"

"Not now. Someone is watching us from the corner."

"Justine's on him," she said, letting him bring his focus back. But she wanted to take care of him first. And that was ridiculous. Security—their security—was the most important thing.

This was the first time she'd been tempted to forget that. "Is he coming with us?" she asked.

"Yes," Daniel said. "Corbin, this is Charity—she's going to free you. Do you have the strength to get out of here?"

Corbin nodded at Daniel.

"He's going to be dead weight—can you handle that?" Daniel asked. For all her height and strength, a man's dead weight was a lot to bear.

"Of course."

She cut the man down and caught him as he slumped forward. His weight made her sag for a second, but then he straightened and held his hands out for her to cut them free. She did it quickly and saw that he was in worse shape than Daniel was.

She keyed her wireless mike. "We need medical."

"Not a problem. I'll be there with the first-aid kit," Anna said. "There's some activity near your car. I think they know you're here."

"I know they do," Charity said.

"What's the plan?"

She turned to Daniel. Her first thought was to leave Corbin tucked away somewhere because he'd slow them down and Daniel was her client. But she didn't know how he'd feel about that.

"Got any ideas about how to get out of here? The girls are covering us, but there's the guard in the corner and at least four others that we know of. And he's going to slow us down."

"Leave me. Take Corbin and get him out of here."

She shook her head, watching Daniel. "I'm *your* body-guard."

"Now you're his. Get him out of here. That's an order."

She started to argue. "Charity, you're an employee of mine, nothing more. You still work for me."

She drew back, fighting the urge to punch him for talking to her that way. Her emotions were ricocheting out of control. She took a deep breath and reminded herself that this was just a job and Daniel was only a client.

"We can argue about this later. For now, we're all getting out of here."

"Charity—"

"Daniel, you hired me to do a job and it's about time I focused on that."

"You help Corbin. I'll make sure we're clear."

She scanned the room, seeing nothing from the corner they'd dispatched Justine to. She motioned for Daniel to follow her.

She heard him curse as she led the way out of the office.

"I can walk," Corbin said as soon as they were outside the office area.

"Save it until you have to," Daniel said, hating everything about this situation. What the hell was wrong with Charity? Didn't she understand that he needed her to be safe?

"If you're given an order, don't argue, just do what your told, okay?"

Corbin nodded. Daniel had the spare gun that Charity had given him in the office and he was hyper-aware of his surroundings. He knew that whatever the reason was for Sekijima leaving, it would have been frivolous, and the other man would be back soon.

Charity moved like the professional she was—they were both here to do a job. Of course, she was trying to save his life, and he was here to make sure that Sekijima stayed dead this time.

Charity motioned them down and he grabbed Corbin's arm and drew the man down toward the floor, searching for cover as Charity swept her gun left and right. She went back to the left, narrowed her eyes, and fired. He heard no sound but the impact of the bullet.

He knew she'd hit whoever was hiding back there but they didn't cry out. There was an immediate return fire, and Charity dove for the ground, rolling until she was in position behind a metal storage container.

She motioned that she'd cover them and laid down some cover fire while he and Corbin ran for her position. Running made his thigh hurt like a bitch—the wound opened and blood was once again dripping down his leg.

"Fuck."

"What?" Charity asked in a soundless whisper, not turning her gaze away from the warehouse floor. "Are you hit?"

"Earlier," he said from between his teeth. He fought to grab her arm and pull her back further into the cover of the container. This was one situation he'd never been in before—in a shoot-out in the past, he'd only cared about himself.

He wouldn't give a fuck who died as long as his enemy was not breathing and he could walk away. But he felt . . . oh, what the hell was this? Fear? Yes, he feared for Charity. And it was making it damned impossible to concentrate as he should.

"Daniel?"

"Hmm?"

"I asked you if you can bind your wound."

"We don't have time." He wasn't going to die from the blood loss. He'd fought in worst shape than this, and he always survived. There was a bit of the cockroach in him, he thought. No matter what, he always continued to exist.

"If you lose too much blood and pass out, it'll be worse," she bit out from between her teeth. "And as you pointed out, you hired me to do a job."

"Dammit, woman, we don't have time—"

"I'm not moving until your wound is bandaged. I can't carry both of you out."

He knew she'd stay put. He heard the stubbornness in her voice. "Give me your knife."

She handed it to him without taking her gaze off the warehouse and the open area. He felt nothing but pure admiration for the soldier that she was. He understood the complete faith that Sam Liberty had in Charity. It was plain to see from the way she held herself that she was simply the best.

"Corbin, help him. Tear his shirt into strips and wrap the wound. Do we need to cut off your pants?"

"No. Find out who's firing on us. I've got this."

"Fine. Just make sure it's done properly."

"It will be."

She leaned out around the storage container and no shots came back at her. "I don't like this."

"I don't, either."

"What don't you like?" Corbin said. He cut a rough strip with Charity's knife.

"The fact that they stopped firing."

"Um . . . that's a good thing; we don't want to be shot at."

"Why did they stop?" Charity asked.

Daniel helped Corbin tie the bandage on his thigh. "The shooter is waiting for something," Daniel said.

"That's some ink you've got there, Daniel."

"It's nothing," he said to Corbin. He didn't want to discuss the tattoo or any of its implications. Even Corbin had to know that kind of artwork wasn't found on just anyone.

"Or someone," Charity said. "Is Sekijima on his way back?"

"That'd be my guess. He wants to kill me himself. But first he needs some information from me." With his shirt off he felt himself sinking back into who he really was. The past wrapped around him and he felt his mind shift into Yakuza mode. Ruthless mode. He was a man who knew what the future held, and it was a killing calm that overtook him.

"What kind?"

The kind that would alienate her from him forever. Not that he had a chance in hell of seeing her again after this, but he kind of liked the idea of a future, or, at the very least, a few more nights in her arms.

"The kind that men die for," he said.

The large warehouse door opened and a car pulled into the open space. Charity gasped and brought her gun up into position.

"What is it?"

"That's Justine's car."

Justine was pushed from the car, blood welling from cuts on her arms and wounds on her face. She was hog-tied, her hands and feet bound together. Sekijima stepped out of the car and kicked her body out of the way.

Daniel felt the waves of rage rolling off of Charity and knew she was going to Sekijima without a second thought. But he couldn't let her do that just yet.

Chapter Twenty

The good you do today may be quickly forgotten, but
the impact of what you do will never disappear.
—Anonymous

Daniel knew there was only one thing he could do and still live with himself and that was to ensure that Charity made it out of this warehouse alive. For the first time in his entire life he had something he wanted more than his own survival. The impact of saving Charity would echo deep inside him in that empty space that she'd somehow made him realize he had.

Sekijima drew his gun and held it pointed at Justine's head. He heard no gasp from Charity, but then she was a professional. Instead he heard her moving around and he knew she was finding a better position from which to fire.

"I'm waiting, Daniel," Sekijima said.

Daniel glanced at Charity and she nodded to say she would be okay. Corbin looked terrified but there was little he could do to help the other man. Daniel wanted to kiss Charity before he left; if things didn't go the way he hoped they would, he wanted to die with her taste on his lips. But there was no time.

"Daniel."

He walked out of the shadows, the semiautomatic pistol held loosely in his left hand. He was bare-chested and ached like hell and was probably in one of the worst situations he'd ever been in, but he was filled with determination.

Sekijima had won the last battle between the two of them. But from this moment on, Daniel was going to be victorious. And this time when he killed the bastard, he was going to make damn sure that Sekijima stayed in Hell.

"Sekijima," he said.

"That's Oyabun to you."

Fuck that. He had hoped to talk things out with Sekijima, find a way to lull him into a sense of false calm.

"Not to me. I'm not your lapdog any more."

"You will be."

Daniel didn't argue. He glanced down at Justine but she didn't meet his gaze. He could feel her rage and he had the feeling that when she got free, she was going to kick some serious ass.

"I'm not getting into bed with you again. I've made a new life for myself." But had he? Until he'd met Charity, he hadn't realized how empty his life was or that his new life was as much a place to hide as his life in the Yakuza had been. He still wasn't really living. How could he, until he put the past to bed?

Justine was working her hands against the rope that bound her. Daniel didn't look at her but he could tell she was making progress.

"A new life," Sekijima said with a sneer. "It's a house of cards—you should realize by now how easily I tore it down. In one day, Daniel. One day."

Sekijima drew his foot back and kicked Justine hard in the ribs. She gasped as all the air rushed from her lungs. Daniel knew that hurt—he had been kicked that way before. "Stop moving, bitch, or I'll kill you now."

"Why are you keeping her alive?" Daniel asked, because it wasn't something Sekijima would have done in the past. And he wanted Justine to realize the man was ruthless. He didn't think she'd need the reminder, but it might help to clarify what she was up against.

"Leverage."

"Leverage? I could give a crap about her," Daniel said.

"Not for you, Daniel. For your bodyguard."

Charity again. Why did Sekijima know that she was the key to making him really suffer? Was it that long-ago bond of brotherhood that gave the other man some insight into him?

"Don't be fooled by the way she looks—she's not the sentimental kind."

"She's a woman, no matter how hard she might want to deny it," Sekijima said. "And the wounds on this one will only get worse until I have both of her partners."

Daniel knew Charity wouldn't give herself up. And Sekijima would know that. He had no way to warn her.

"What do you want from me?" Daniel asked at last. He wanted to hear it from Sekijima's own lips.

"I want you to honor the ink on your body. Those tattoos came with a promise, and you broke it. You dishonored everything that you once were. You know the penalty for that."

"That's old news, Sekijima. I thought we'd moved beyond that. What do you want now?"

"Money. And this enterprise put back in the Dragon Lords."

Daniel would give up the money—it meant little to him. Rich or poor, his life had always been about survival. "That's it?"

"I also want your life. I'm going to enjoy torturing you. Then I'm going to leave you for dead, Daniel. But unlike you, I'm going to sit and patiently wait for the blood to drain from your beaten body."

Daniel knew that Sekijima was capable of doing just that. "I'm not easy to kill."

"Nothing is ever easy in this life," Sekijima said, and those were words Daniel had heard more than once in his life. He knew what they meant and how living a hard life changed a

man. It had been at the heart of the bond between him and
Sekijima.

And for a moment, Sekijima wasn't his enemy—he was the
brother that Daniel remembered from long ago. The man
who'd had so much in common with him.

"So if the girl is for the bodyguard, what are you going to
use to get my cooperation?"

"The bodyguard," Sekijima said.

"She means nothing to me."

"Yet you have taken her."

"She was convenient."

"Convenient? Possibly, but you're more particular than
that."

Daniel knew he should have kept his hands to himself.
Knew that with all that was going on, Charity had come into
his life at the worst possible time. "She was a woman, Sekijima. You know they mean nothing to me."

"Perhaps. We'll see when I have her."

Daniel fought not to react to Sekijima. He wanted to raise
his gun and empty the magazine into the other man, then rip
his throat from his body. The rage was so overwhelming that
he wasn't sure he was masking his reaction.

Sekijima brought the butt of his gun down on Justine's
head and the woman was knocked unconscious. "That's better. She was getting on my nerves, trying to free herself."

"Survival is an instinct, Sekijima. You know that."

"So is love."

"I don't love anyone."

"That used to be true but we'll see if it still is."

Charity disappeared into the shadows while Daniel and Sekijima confronted each other. It was way harder than she wanted
to admit to see Justine bound the way she was. They'd been
in tough spots before as a team but this was by far the tough-
est.

"How the hell did he get Justine?" Charity asked Anna via the wireless earpiece.

"I'm not sure. She went silent to go after the guy in the corner. There's two men outside and I've got my sniper rifle trained on Sekijima. Should I take him out?"

"Hold. Let me get the two outside. If he tries to shoot Daniel or Justine, take him."

"Sounds good. I need another set of eyes. The last position I had on them was to the north of you."

"And the other one?"

"Circling from the other side."

"I've got a civilian here," Charity said.

"Can he shoot? Because we could use another gun."

"Give me a minute."

Charity turned to Corbin, who was pale, sweating, and clearly at his wit's end. "How you doing?"

"Fine."

She had good instincts with people and her gut said that Corbin would do what he needed to. "Dammit, Anna. I don't have another weapon."

"What happened to your spare?"

"Daniel."

"Got it. We have a bunch of stuff in Justine's car. I can't believe that bloody wanker got her ride."

"Me, either," Charity said. "Corbin, stay here. No matter what you see. Staying hidden is the only thing that can keep you alive at this point."

He nodded. "I can help."

"I know."

"Do you think Justine's really out?" Anna asked in her ear.

"I'm not sure. I'm hoping she's faking until we need her . . . but wait a minute."

Charity turned back to Corbin. "Do you think you can stay low and get to Justine?"

"Ah, what?"

"If you stick to the shadows and crawl under the car," Charity said.

Corbin looked scared. "She's got her earpiece in, so all you'd have to do is pass the knife to her when she moves her fingers," Charity continued.

"She can't say anything," Anna reminded her.

"It's the only chance we have. We need her."

"Okay. I'll cover him from here. But . . ."

"I know," Charity said. Anna didn't have to say it: Corbin was expendable. They weren't going to give him up without a fight, but if it came down to him or Justine or him or Daniel, Anna would have to sacrifice him.

"Corbin, this is a risky thing to do. There's a chance you could be caught."

"What else are they going to do to me? I'm beat to hell and sitting here while a woman tries to save the day . . ."

"I'm not just a woman, I'm trained for this. And I'm not going to *try* to save the day, Corbin. I'm going to."

"Then I want to help," he said.

She smiled at him and handed over her switchblade. "If you have to use this, get close and stab deep. The best place would be the groin or gut."

"Okay. How will I know if she's ready for the knife?"

"She'll move her fingers. Slide it to her blade-first, then roll out of the way. They are going to come after you, so run like hell for cover and stay put until I come for you. Or the cops do—don't trust anyone else."

"Okay. I won't let you down."

"I know you won't," Charity said, knowing a confident man would be better than someone who wasn't sure she was counting on him.

"Tell Justine when you see Corbin get into position," Charity said to Anna.

"I will."

"Come on, Corbin. I'll be with you until we reach the door."

Corbin was quiet for someone with no training. He was also nervous, and she felt him shaking as she touched his back. When they got to the door, she realized there was about five feet of open space where Corbin would be visible. The driver was still behind the wheel of the car.

From the tense way he sat, she knew he was watching and waiting for her. "Do you think they know how many of us there are?"

"I have no idea. I'm trying to listen in to the conversation down there—it seems he's just baiting Daniel. He wants to torture you, Charity. So be careful."

"I will be. I'm not planning to let myself be used."

"Oh, God."

"What?"

"He's going to use Justine to get you."

"He doesn't know about Corbin . . . he's our ace in the hole."

"I am?"

"He is?"

"Yes. I'm going to let the driver see me, Anna—let him come after me. When he does, Corbin, you get under the car, quick and quiet."

He nodded.

"I don't like it. There's already two men outside and we don't know where they are exactly," Anna said.

"I can handle them. They are just men," Charity said, using Justine's favorite expression.

"Not you, too," Anna said, but Charity knew her friend appreciated the reminder that the three of them had gotten the better of many men. "We're women, not Amazons."

"I'm going to tell Justine you said that."

Charity moved quickly, keeping to the shadows. A part of

her, a really big part of her, hated letting Anna watch Daniel's back, but Charity was the only one who could make certain they only had Sekijima to deal with.

Charity didn't think about what she was doing. She only acted on instinct. She knew she had a pretty good chance of not getting shot by the driver. She was quick and had run this scenario before. Sam always set them up in situations like this at their yearly retreat. They had to take the hit or the shot to escape.

"Ready, Anna?"

"Whenever you are."

She got herself where she needed to be mentally, thinking of herself as nothing more than a tool, a weapon that would be used to save the lives of two people. She couldn't think of how much she cared for them because that would shake her focus.

She put on a burst of speed running out of the shadows. A split second later she heard the car door open and the sound of pursuit. She also heard a rapid gunshot. Sekijima's gun. Dammit, she hoped that Corbin wasn't hit, but she couldn't pause to make sure he was okay.

She had to do her job—take out the three other men circling the building.

She felt the whiz of a bullet going past her on the left and dropped into a crouch, rolling behind the Dumpster at the side of the building. Her breathing wasn't accelerated but she'd practiced for years to regulate it, even when she exercised.

The area outside the warehouse was illuminated by high-pressure, sodium-vapor security lighting every fifteen feet, leaving very little room for her to hide. The smell of rotting trash nearly overpowered her, but she tucked that away.

Her body ached from the punches she'd taken earlier when fighting with Amanda. She really wanted to keep this clean and quick. The driver was behind her somewhere, and if Sekijima was half the leader she knew he was, one of his other guys would be waiting for her to take her shot at the driver.

And then they'd get her. She had to be smart about this. It would be easier to do this from a higher position. She looked at the wall—solid concrete would be impossible to climb.

Dammit, she was wasting time. Justine could be dead, or even Daniel. She had to get moving.

She wished she had her second gun, but with only one, and guessing that she'd have two adversaries set up to fire on her, she'd have to take the first shot and then roll over and take the second one. Which was risky, really. Her other option was . . . she looked around the area, trying to see if there was anything else she could use as a weapon.

She could use the wall for support for a running wall kick and knock out the first guy. She took a deep breath, gauging the wall and where she'd need to hit it, and then she intentionally stepped back into the trash can, making a slight scraping noise.

The driver moved toward her position and she ran past him, gaining momentum, then ran her right foot up the wall. She kicked through the turn to keep her momentum as the driver stepped forward and brought his gun up toward her.

She swung around toward him, kicking at his carotid artery with her right foot, using the heel of her boot to drop him. He fell to the ground, his gun dropping a few feet from his body. She landed on both feet and dropped into a shooting crouch just as a bullet hit her in the right shoulder. She bit back a cry of pain, and raised her own weapon, squeezing off two quick shots. She heard the solid thud of a body hitting the ground.

She shoved the driver's gun into the holster at the small of her back and removed the flex cuffs from her pocket, binding his hands and then his feet and then gagging him. She muscled his body over behind the Dumpster, then grabbed the second shooter, who was dead. She aimed true, not wounding him, because wounded men could still kill; dead men couldn't.

She dragged the body out of the lit area and checked in with Anna.

"Two down out here. Everything okay inside?"

"No. Corbin's down. Dead, I think."

"Dammit."

"Daniel shot Sekijima in the shoulder as he turned. He's now bound by his wrists, and Sekijima is beating him. I'm not sure how much longer he can take it."

"Justine?"

"She's strung up as well, but she's not out of it. She looks so pissed off."

"I don't know where the other man is out here. I need to take care of him."

"Time is of the essence," Anna said.

"I know. Can you shoot Justine down?"

"Maybe. She's unarmed."

"But not weaponless," Charity said.

"I'll do it," Anna said. "On three, Justine, be ready."

With Justine's hair cut in a bob, the earpiece was practically invisible to the naked eye, and the earpieces they used were tiny.

"I'm coming back to the warehouse—I'm betting the last guy will come in when he hears the gunshots. And I can take care of freeing Daniel," Charity said.

"Are you sure?"

"It's the only thing that makes sense. I can't just run around out here while they're being beaten."

"No, you can't."

"Who else is with Sekijima?"

"A woman. She's tall—taller than you, Charity—and she's quick. And vicious."

"As soon as we free them, I'll take Sekijima, you take the girl," Charity said.

"Okay, tell me when you're in position."

Charity made her way carefully back to the warehouse, still sticking to the shadows, knowing that there was another man out here somewhere.

Daniel looked like hell, she thought, as she stared in at him. Her heart skipped a beat. Sekijima was totally ruthless in the way he was torturing Daniel, and it was nothing less than torture.

She felt that rage well up once again and the sound that emerged from her throat was a cry of rage.

Chapter Twenty-one

You must learn to be still in the midst of activity.
—Indira Gandhi

Daniel knew he'd let things get out of control, but he was in control now. The next time Sekijima came close enough to punch him, he'd grab the other man with his legs and choke him. He was pretty sure that Charity would be back to cover him, and he could strangle Sekijima in the time it took Suki to get her weapon at the ready.

He gripped the rope with his hands, readying himself to move. His fingers were a little slippery with blood that dripped from the wound he'd made trying to cut himself free.

But he had fought in worse conditions and walked away. After seeing Charity shot at, and the fear that he'd felt for her, he knew he had to end this.

Sekijima shook his head as he stepped forward one more time.

"This is pointless," Daniel said. "Cut the girl down—she's not going to be valuable to you as leverage if she's dead."

Either Justine was a hell of an actress or the woman was about two seconds from passing out. She was pale and had lost more blood than he had. She'd struggled with Sekijima and Suki, which had just pissed the pair off.

"Death is where we are both most comfortable, Daniel."

Was that still true? He knew for a long time he had been

most comfortable around death. It had made him feel powerful to take a life. To have the power of deciding when an
enemy would leave this world.

But now he felt empty inside at the lives he'd ruined and
the futures he'd altered.

"We don't know each other anymore, Sekijima. The Oyabun that I served was a man who lived his life by his own
code."

"Indeed I did. What changed?"

"You did. Your family would never have approved of the
way you stopped valuing all life."

"That's why I'm the only one still standing, Daniel. There
are always sacrifices that must be made for prosperity and survival."

Daniel tightened his arms and kicked out with his left leg,
catching Sekijima off guard. Sekijima danced out of range.

The sound of a bullet ripped through the warehouse and he
felt the impact in the rope above his hands. The threads un-
raveled quickly and he bent his knees, knowing he was going
to hit the ground. He rolled with the momentum of his fall
and came up ready for the punch that Sekijima delivered to
his chest.

Daniel staggered back, found his balance, and lashed out
with a strong upper kick to Sekijima's face. The other man's
head snapped back and blood spurted from his nose.

Daniel kept up his forward assault, using the martial arts
skills he'd learned in Sekijima's family's dojo to drive the
other man back.

He remembered the cool way that Sekijima had ordered
Charity to be found and then killed, because otherwise it was
all too easy to see the face of his friend instead of his enemy in
the man standing before him.

Justine was indeed a better actress than he gave her credit
for. She was engaged with Suki a few feet from Daniel. Fighting for her life and bringing the other woman down.

Sekijima brought his gun up and Daniel bent low, head-butting the other man in the gut, driving him back with all the rage and frustration he'd felt for so long.

All the injustices he'd witnessed and perpetrated boiled up inside him and he knew that it had to end tonight. Now.

He drove Sekijima into the side of the car. The abrupt stop knocked him off balance and Sekijima brought his fist with the gun hard against the side of Daniel's head.

Daniel laced his fingers together and brought his hands up to Sekijima's face, knocking him off balance, then grabbing his gun. Sekijima pulled the trigger and the impact jarred Daniel but he kept his grip on his opponent's gun hand.

Sekijima lifted his arm over his head and Daniel jerked hard and brought his knee up hard, aiming for Sekijima's groin.

He hit the other man hard, but there was no reaction save for a strong exhalation of breath. Sekijima pushed hard on the wound in his thigh, digging with the fingers of his free hand.

Daniel struggled to stay on his feet and not lose his grip on the gun hand. Behind him he knew the women battled it out, but he concentrated on his fight.

On bringing Sekijima to his knees.

He jerked them both backward, twisting hard on the hand holding the gun as Sekijima tried to shift his hand in Daniel's grip. Daniel stepped forward with his right leg, turning his right shoulder in toward Sekijima. He lowered his stance, driving Sekijima off balance, and threw him over his shoulder.

Daniel followed him down, jumping on top of Sekijima's body and bringing his bound hands under Sekijima's head. He drew his hands to the left under Sekijima's chin, bringing his forearm against the other man's windpipe. Sekijima bucked against Daniel, who braced his feet on the cement floor and held on.

He drew his arms back until his grip tightened against Sekijima's head. In his periphery, he saw Sekijima bringing up his gun hand.

Daniel didn't hesitate—he pulled hard to the left, lifting Sekijima's head and breaking his neck.

He stayed where he was on top of Sekijima's body, freeing the other man's neck only when he was certain that no breath was left in Sekijima's body. He stood up and reached for the gun, wanting to ensure that this time his enemy didn't come back from the dead.

"Daniel, he's gone."

Charity's voice was deep and husky. He wondered if she was disgusted by the man she'd given herself to. There was no hiding behind his civilized exterior anymore. She saw him as he was. Shirt off with his Yakuza tattoos visible. Bloodied and beaten, gun in his hand, and he'd just killed a man.

"This is what I never wanted you to see," he said, realizing that for once he was speaking the truth. And it mattered to him that she understand this. "My life . . . this is my life. No matter how far I run, it always comes back to this."

Charity didn't say anything, just stepped forward. She lifted his bound hands and slid her body underneath them. Her arms came around his waist and she held him close.

He rubbed his hands against her back, then dipped low to find her lips with his. Deep inside he thanked God for the fact that he'd been able to defeat Sekijima and that Charity was alive and in his arms.

Charity was swamped with emotion and aches and pains, but standing in Daniel's arms soothed that. She knew she'd gone to a dark place deep inside herself tonight.

"The cops are on their way," Anna said. She had her sniper rifle slung over her shoulder and had taken out the last guard on the exterior.

"We need to start cleaning up the scene," Justine said. "Hug Daniel later."

Charity nodded and moved away reluctantly. She couldn't really explain it, but she was afraid that if she didn't reinforce the bond between her and Daniel . . . what was that bond?

He'd said earlier that it was just sex, and now she was cling-
ing to him like that didn't matter. She moved away. "I've got
two guys behind a Dumpster."

"Dead."

"One is."

"I'll help you," Justine said.

"I'll bandage Daniel's leg. I called for EMTs as well."

Charity stopped by Corbin. His pulse was thready but he
was still alive—he moaned a little. Her emotions were hidden
again, deep inside. Deadened by everything that had happened tonight. She wondered if Perry hadn't been right when
he said she played at being a tough-ass.

Because the only way she survived her job was to bury the
true woman underneath a bunch of protective layers.

"Come on, Charity. Let's get those two."

She nodded and pushed to her feet. Justine was a little
worse for wear.

"What the hell happened to you?"

"There were two of them," Justine said. "I thought I had
them, but . . ."

"Hey, it happens to the best of us."

"Yes, it does. So what's up with Daniel? We all heard what
he said to you."

"I don't know. I don't think I can go there yet. I just want to
wrap this up."

"And then?"

"I have no idea. Sam's been pushing me to take some time
off."

"Time off? Is a vacation really going to help?"

"Hell, Justine, I have no idea. I only know that if I go back
to D.C. and—" She broke off, realizing the truth. She wasn't
going to take a vacation. She was going to go right on to the
next case. She needed to stay busy to save her own sanity.

She had to keep moving because if she stood still she was
going to have to deal with the fact that she'd fallen in love

with a man who wasn't what she'd expected. A man who didn't fit the nice, safe mold that she'd always thought she wanted.

There was a reason why she'd thought Senator Perry was the man for her, and it was deeply rooted in the fact that she had never really liked herself. Not all of who she was, anyway. But there was no hiding from that now. That vigilante part had been reawakened tonight and she knew that she didn't want to shove her back into a box.

"I'm not going on vacation. That's not what I need."

"Damn straight. Work is the only thing women like us can count on."

"True enough," Charity said. They reached the Dumpster and Justine pulled the man who was still alive to his feet and marched him toward the warehouse. Charity bent low and pulled the deceased man over her shoulders, fireman style.

The weight was heavy but manageable. She knew that this man had a family and loved ones who would be distraught by the fact that he wasn't coming home again. But a part of her couldn't regret his death. He would have killed her and her team. And her client.

The only thing that she was really confident of was her competence as a bodyguard. This was a little messier than she anticipated, but she'd done the job she needed to do.

She walked into the warehouse and slid the body onto the floor next to Sekijima and Suki. The Asian woman had been damned hard to kill and had almost strangled Anna in the process.

Her BlackBerry rang and Charity glanced at the caller ID before answering. "Hey, Sam."

"Hey, girl. Everything okay on your end?"

"Well, Daniel's alive, his blackmailer is dead and the cops are on the way. As I'm sure you know, since Anna probably text-messaged you as soon as she got off the phone with the police."

"Before, actually," Sam said. His voice was deep and soothing. She'd always liked his voice, and to be honest, wondered about the man behind it. "I was asking about you, not the case."

"Me? I'm fine."

"Charity, you don't sound fine."

"Sam—don't, okay? I'm fine and let's leave it at that."

"Very well. Are you taking any time off?"

"Ah, no."

The cops arrived, sirens blarring and guns drawn. "Gotta go."

She hung up the phone.

Two weeks later, Daniel was back in D.C. on business, testifying once again on the Hill and going about his normal routine as if his life hadn't been radically changed. He hadn't heard from Charity since she'd walked out of the warehouse with the rest of her team.

He'd been taken to the hospital, his wounds treated, and then released. Corbin was on an extended vacation, and Alonzo had resigned his position, deciding that Daniel wasn't worth taking a bullet for. He'd called Sam Liberty and closed out his case with them.

Daniel had wanted to ask about Charity but in the end he hadn't been able to. What did a man who was nothing but a shill for violence and destruction have to offer a woman like her?

He'd searched deep inside himself and in the end had made the sacrifice of his own happiness for hers. Because he knew he'd never be able to have Charity and let her be the woman she was.

If she was his, he'd demand she give up her job and try to put her on a pedestal so he could protect her. He never wanted to see her bruised or bleeding again. And the way he felt about that was so damned strong, he'd taken the high road and pretended that she hadn't taken whatever bit of a soul he'd had.

But dammit, he missed her. Which was fucking stupid be-cause he'd only had her in his life for one day. One damned day, and she'd totally rocked his world.

He stood in the suite at the Marquis, staring at the window and searching for a way to a future. Any future where he could be with Charity.

If she'd even have him, and there was no guarantee that she would.

"What happened to your temporary employee?" Tobias asked, coming into the living room from the hall.

"She was temporary."

"You know I don't give you advice," Tobias said.

"Uh, yeah."

"There was something different about her," Tobias said.

"She's a goddess, Tobias. And you're a mortal, so of course you'd find something different about her."

"I meant with you. You were different with her. Not so cold . . . more alive."

"Your point?"

"We only live once, and whatever was in your past . . . well, it's time to let it go."

Daniel turned the conversation back to work, but early that evening when Tobias left and he realized he was faced with an evening alone, he thought about Charity again.

He wanted her. And not just because he was in D.C. He wanted her in his life because when he looked at the future he saw all the long, empty years stretching out in front of him.

And when he looked to the past, he saw the same empti-ness except for one crazy day when he'd had her in his life.

He pulled his BlackBerry from his pocket and dialed Sam Liberty's number.

"Daniel, what can I do for you?" Sam asked.

"I need a favor."

"Anything for a client."

"Um . . . this isn't about business."

There was silence on the line.

"Charity?" Sam asked.

"Yes. I know . . . listen, I just need to see her. To talk to her, and I wondered if you would give me her home address."

Sam didn't say anything, but Daniel heard the clicking of a computer keyboard. "I can't do that, but go to the Liberty Investigations office and I'll have her meet you there."

"An office?"

"That's all I can do for you, Daniel."

Daniel didn't care where he met Charity, as long as he could see her again. Then he'd know if he had just imagined the intensity of everything she'd made him feel or if it was. And then once he knew it was real, he was going to claim her. And he could do that anywhere.

Chapter Twenty-two

To train the mind, you must exercise the patience
and determination it takes to shape that steel.
— The Dalai Lama

Charity wasn't in the best mood as she entered the offices of Liberty Investigations. It was eight o'clock on a Saturday night and she had a date with BBC-America and *Dr. Who*. But when Sam called, she didn't argue. The same box of Celestial Seasonings Raspberry Zinger tea sat in the kitchen and she made herself a quick cup while she waited for the rest of the team to arrive.

She and the Dalai Lama still weren't back on the same wavelength. But then, nothing Zen had been happening for her since she'd left Daniel in Seattle.

She knew from what Sam said that he'd recovered from his wounds and was back to work. Back to his life. A life that she didn't really fit into. Guarding Daniel had changed her—she no longer felt half alive anymore.

"Now I feel dead *all* the time," she muttered. God, she was getting morose, which she couldn't stand.

She took her tea and walked out into the hallway when she heard the airtight door open with a beep. She froze as she recognized Daniel standing in the doorway. He stepped inside and let the door close behind him.

"What are you doing here?"

"I came to see you," he said.

"Are you still being blackmailed?" she asked, focusing on the business that had been between them because the little thrill she'd felt at his words wasn't comfortable. She didn't like to think about how many nights she'd laid awake longing to feel his arms around her once again.

"No. Everything's going good with my business."

"That's great. So why are you here?"

"For you. I know you heard me say that."

"I don't know what that means, Daniel."

He closed the gap between them and took the tea mug out of her hands, reaching around her to put it on the counter in the kitchen. "It means that I needed to see you again and ascertain that what I felt for you wasn't a dream."

She was afraid to let him continue. All she'd wanted was for him to come back into her life, and she knew she wasn't going to deal well if he was back for sex and nothing more.

"A sexy dream?"

"Well, that's part of it, but it was more how completely you fit into my life. I know that I'm not much of a catch as a man . . ."

"Daniel, you're a wonderful man. You know I admire what you've made of your life. How you came from nothing . . . please don't say that you're not much of a catch."

"Do you really believe that stuff?" he asked.

"Yes. I do."

"But I'm still a Yakuza street punk deep inside. That mark will always be on my body and in my mind."

"You're also a CEO and that is also a mark you wear. I admire that you have melded those two parts of yourself. I've never been able to."

He drew her into his arms. "That's because you've never let any man know both sides of the complex and beautiful woman you are."

She rested her head on his shoulder for just a second. "Why are you here?"

"Because I want you."

"Sex?"

"Love," he said. "My life has always been solitary and I've been okay with that, but you gave me a brief glimpse of what it could be and I find that I want more of it."

"I'm not like other women."

"Which is precisely why I love you."

"You love me?"

"Yes, I do. And I've never loved anything. But you I can't get out of my mind, Charity. You are in my heart and soul and I'm desperate to meld our lives together."

Charity's breath caught in her throat. "Oh, Daniel, I want that as well. You're the first man who's seen every part of me and accepted it."

She thought of the gift that Daniel was offering her. All she had to do was believe him. Believe in the love he said he felt for her. And she knew without him saying anything else that she already loved him. "I love you, too, Daniel."

"How can you? I'm a street punk, even dressed in these clothes."

"I love everything that makes you who you are."

Daniel pulled her close and kissed her slowly and deeply. She wrapped her arms around him and held him tightly, realizing that she'd found the home she'd been searching for since her parents' deaths long ago.

And she'd found that home here in Daniel's arms. They left the office and went back to his suite, where they made love all night and made plans for the future.

Try another one of Brava's hot titles,
like Shannon McKenna's
EXTREME DANGER,
new this month.
Turn the page for a sneak peek!

"C-c-can we just, um, establish here and now that I am no bodily threat to you?" she squeaked. "Cross my heart. All I did was trespass. It was stupid. I'm sorry. It will never happen again. The gun, the cuffs, this interrogation routine, it all strikes me as, um . . . overkill?"

A menacing grin flashed across his face. "Does it strike you that way?" he crooned. He was so close, the surface of his body touched the tips of her breasts. The swell of her belly. The points of contact seemed to burn. Her lips were so close to the hollow of his collarbone, the swatch of smooth black body hair that disappeared into his shirt. "Maybe you're right," he added softly. "Only time will tell."

"H-h-how much time?" she stuttered. "You're trying to intimidate me, buddy. I do not appreciate it. One bit."

"Trying? I thought I was succeeding. I must be losing my touch."

She gulped. "It's not working," she lied. "It's falling very flat."

He glanced down. Her puckered nipples brushed his chest, as softly as a kiss. The heat of his erection jutted against the curve of her belly. Scorching her. Sweat broke out on her face. Her heart thudded.

"Doesn't look flat to me," he murmured. "The landscape looks pretty rugged, from where I'm standing."

"Step away from me, right now," she whispered. "Give me space."

A frown creased his brow. He stepped back, to her amazement. Cold displaced the buzzing force field emanating from his body. She felt exposed, vulnerable. She wrapped her arms around herself.

He grabbed them, and flung them wide. "Don't," he said. "You wanted to be more adventurous, right? So stand up straight. Stop cringing. No wonder your boyfriend ran around on you. Would Kaia 'the bitch' slut cower and cringe?"

She gasped. Her back straightened, her chin lifted, her breasts tilted as she hiked her ribcage up. "Go to hell," she hissed.

It was becoming ever more obvious that he was aroused. His loose raggedy cargo pants hid nothing. He was naked beneath them, and getting bigger by the second. He noticed the direction of her gaze, and jerked his chin, with a you-wanna-make-something-of-it look.

God, did she? Her thighs tingled. She wondered, out of the blue, how it would feel to, ah, accommodate a man of those proportions.

He was picturing that scenario, too. She saw it in his eyes. Fear and excitement jolted over her. Oh, boy. Oh, dear.

Things are about to get electric in
COSMIC SEX,
the latest book from Karen Kelley,
out this month from Brava . . .

"I don't have anything to eat. We can stop at a Micky D's for breakfast."

From the confused look on her face, he didn't think she even knew what a McDonald's was. His amnesia theory was starting to make a lot more sense. "I just have to get my wallet."

Nick hurried to the bedroom but there was a pop as he reached the place where his door used to be. His head smacked into a hard surface.

His door was back.

Great timing.

He rubbed his forehead.

"She is not an alien. She is not an alien," he mumbled as he opened the door and grabbed his wallet off the dresser.

On the way to the fast-food joint, he covertly observed her every move and noticed how she watched him before repeating what he did. He still hadn't ruled out that she could be from another country.

He parked in front of the fast-food place and they went inside.

"What do you want?" he asked, looking at the menu.

"I've never had food before."

He glanced around. Good thing everyone was busy and no

one had come over to wait on them yet. "You don't eat . . . where you're from?" he asked, keeping his voice down.

"Food capsules. It provides plenty of nourishment, and we don't have to bother with using space to grow anything."

She turned those dark blue eyes on him and his insides began to melt.

"But I'd like to try your food. The soda was quite refreshing."

Hell, he'd give her anything she wanted if she kept looking at him like that. Food, sex . . . state secrets.

He cleared his throat and ordered two pancake breakfasts and two milks, then carried them to a table in the far corner. Keep a low profile, that was the name of the game.

He covertly watched her as she slid into the booth across from him. Man, if she was playing him for a fool and Sam was in on this, he'd kill them both.

She just stared at the white Styrofoam, then pinched off a corner of the lid and put it in her mouth. Before he had a chance to react, she spit it out. "Ugh, your food isn't good."

He quickly glanced around to make sure she hadn't been seen, breathing a sigh of relief. No one was paying them the least bit of attention.

"That's the box," he told her, then opened it and poured syrup over the stack of pancakes. "Like this." He cut into one, then forked it into his mouth. She followed suit.

Her eyes closed, she moaned. The overhead lights began to flash. A bulb popped.

"Mmm . . . this is good. Oh, yes . . . yes!"

Nick's gaze scanned the room. A busload of geriatrics had just come inside. Their expressions ranged from amusement, to reprimanding looks, to fear as some noticed the wild light display above their heads.

"This is so wonderful, Nick." She rolled her shoulders, her back arched, her tight nipples clearly outlined through the material of her top. "I've never had anything this good before."

He realized he was holding his breath when the room began to spin. He exhaled, but continued to stare. She was giving him a major hard-on as her tongue came out to slowly lick the syrup off her lips.

She opened her eyes and forked another bite into her mouth. "I think I love your food, Nick." Her words were raspy, like a woman ready to smear syrup all over his body and lick off every drop.

He grabbed a paper napkin and wiped the sweat from his forehead. That's when his attention was drawn to the lights. They were still flickering, but that wasn't all. A wave of bright blues, yellows, and pinks swirled like the aurora borealis.

Damn, the same thing had happened last night when they'd had sex, but he'd dismissed it as a figment of his imagination. She'd been really hot in the sack and it'd been a while for him so he hadn't really thought much about them. Only that his eyes had to be playing tricks. It had been a really fantastic orgasm.

Kia squirmed in her seat as she shoved another bite in her already stuffed mouth. Syrup drizzled down her chin. She swallowed.

"More. I want more . . . thank you."

She looked like a woman in the throes of passion.

Keep an eye out for HelenKay Dimon's
RIGHT HERE, RIGHT NOW,
coming next month from Brava . . .

"I thought you went home?" Reed asked the question in the friendliest tone he could muster, while his car sat in the direct firing line of Gabby's anger.

"Not yet." She scraped her heel against his fender.

He felt the screeching sound echo down to the pit of his stomach. "Yeah, I see that."

As if sensing his discomfort, she banged her heel a second time.

"Could you not do that?"

"Sit?"

He rubbed his hand over the cool metal and winced when he felt what he feared was a deep scratch. "Vandalize my vehicle."

"Do you have a better target in mind?" Her voice dripped with disgust.

He pulled back until he stood out of kicking range. "So, the idea of this meeting was to finish me off in the middle of the street?"

She stopped watching the front door of the restaurant and started scowling at him. She may have even snarled.

"What, a man can't ask a question?"

"You're making me think that finishing you off has some merit."

Just as he thought. "Maybe we should go back inside."

"Why?"

"Because there are people in there who can act as witnesses and the ambulance is only a call away." He adjusted his earphone to make sure she could not see it.

Pete was not talking but Reed could hear him breathing. Reed hoped his lazy partner also had 911 on speed dial.

"I'm not going anywhere with you."

That was pretty clear, but her comment did not explain everything. "You have me at a disadvantage here, Gabby."

"There's an interesting take on this evening's festivities."

"Uh-oh," Pete whispered on his end.

Reed saw the trap without Pete's help. Making the lovely lady even angrier was not a good plan. If he knew how to prevent that possibility, he would.

"What are you doing out here?"

"Standing."

"On my car?"

"Feeling dramatic, aren't you?"

"You're the one who threw the wine and beat up my car." He cleared his throat in an attempt to send an I-mean-business signal. "And, feel free to jump off it at any time."

She saw his I-mean-business signal and raised him a your-car-is-at-my-mercy look. "After everything that's happened tonight you're telling me the only thing you care about is the vehicle? Typical male."

Did not take a genius level IQ to know the comment was not a compliment. "Did I miss the part where you explained why you're out here?"

"I'm waiting."

That explained . . . nothing. "For me?"

He almost hoped she would say no.

"Yes." She slid off the hood, clanking her heels against the car a few more times before she hit the ground.

"Could you be careful—"

"You have my keys." Her icy tone made the back of his neck itch.

"I do?" He patted his suit pocket but only felt the wet and sticky remnants of his dinner beverage. No keys. "I don't have—"

"They're in your glove compartment."

Sounded plausible even though opening the door meant turning his back on her for a second. "When did you stick them in there?"

"When we parked. They didn't fit in my purse." She waved a square black box in his face.

"Then why buy it?"

Her eyebrow inched up. "Excuse me?"

Words stuttered to a halt in his throat but he forced them out anyway. "Just seems like it would be more practical to carry a bag you can stick crap in."

"Do you really want to have an argument about my accessories right now?"

"That would be tough since I have no idea what that even means." Then he saw the flat line of her lips. "And then there's the part about the lack of witnesses to my potential homicide."

"You might want to keep that in mind."

"I am. Trust me."

Pete's chuckle echoed in the earpiece. "She is so damn hot."

"Get my keys." She said the words like an order.

"You didn't have to wait out here. You could have . . ." Reed was not sure how to end that sentence since a return trip to the table likely would have resulted in more liquor throwing. "Forget it."

"The keys." She held out her palm. "Now."

"Sure." The horn sounded as he hit the unlock button. A few seconds later the glove compartment popped open. "Here you go."

She grabbed her keys but did not move. "I wasn't waiting for you."

"You said you were."

"I lied."

"Man. I'd run," Pete whispered but the warning boomed through the ear speaker and straight into Reed's brain.

Somehow Reed focused on the furious woman in front of him instead of the wise words in his ear. Probably had something to do with the fact Gabby held her keys like a weapon.

"My initial thought was to break your car window and get the keys myself."

So, she thought about using violence. Now there was some bad news. "Lucky for me you came up with a second option."

"Not yet." She pursed her lips together as if thinking of her next move or how best to kill him. "I want you to understand something."

That he was a dead man? Yeah. He got that part. "Which is?"

"What you gave up." She dropped her keys on the hood.

"Hey, be careful—"

When her lips covered his, he stopped talking. Stopped thinking. Stop giving a damn about his car. She took his breath until he had nothing left. Including common sense.